I0744090

Cold SPELL

Sweet Escape Series – Book Three

MIA LONDON & SUSAN SHEEHEY

AMEPPHIRE PRESS

Cold Spell
Sweet Escape Series
Book Three
by Mia London and Susan Sheehey

This is a work of fiction. Names, characters, places and incidents either are the product of the author's imagination or are used factitiously, and any resemblance to actual persons, living or dead, business establishments, event or locales is entirely coincidental.
Reference to Belinda Carlisle is purely fictional. We adore her, and if at any point she would like a copy, we are happy to send her a signed paperback.

Copyright © 2018 Mia London & Susan Sheehey

ISBN: 978-1947874121 (E-Book)
978-1947874152 (paperback)

Publisher: Amepphire Press
11923 NE Sumner St, Ste 766015
Portland, OR 97220

Edited by Traci Hall
Formatted by Formatting by Leigh Stone
Cover design copyright © L.J. Anderson, Mayhem Cover Creations

Dedication

To all the hard-working mothers, wives, and sisters everywhere.

Whether a nurse, a banker, a teacher, an oil rig manager, we dedicate this to you all.

Your devotion to family, work, and doing the right thing, even when it's not easy, are to be commended.

We see you, we raise our glass to you, and thank you.

Other novels
BY MIA & SUSAN

Other Novels by Mia London & Susan Sheehey

Dry Spell

Hot Spell

Cold Spell

Other Novels by Mia London

Undeniable Series

Undeniable Fate

Undeniable Love

Perfect Series

Perfect Seduction

Perfect Surrender

Life To The Max

Wanton Angel *(Prequel to Life To The Max)*

Beyond Lace (Hard Men of the Rockies 4)

Other Novels by Susan Sheehey

Royals of Solana Series

Prince of Solana

Jewel of Solana

Crown of Solana

Royal Wedding novella

Knights of Texas Series

Tell Me What You Want

Tell Me What You Crave

Tell Me What You Need

Tell Me What You Feel

Audrey's Promise

Chapter ONE

THE RAIN SLAPPED against Liddy's apartment window—dark and dreary—like her mood.

San Francisco's five straight days of rain covered the whole city in a dismal cloud. Meteorologists predicted at least three more days.

Ugh. Was *ugh* a mood? Because if so, that had been her mantra over the last week.

Everything was constantly wet. She'd step into work at the designer boutique shop, and have wet shoes all day, topped off with matted hair. She'd come home, strip out of her wet clothes, and veg in front of the TV.

God bless sweatpants!

When will this rain ever end?

Every northern California resident who lived there any significant amount of time, knew rainy season started in November. So, she shouldn't be surprised. Didn't mean she had to like it. *Ugh.*

She shot a return text her friend, Sam, who'd asked if she

could borrow Liddy's black mini Coach handbag for some event she and Chase had that Sunday.

Sure. She didn't need it.

She had no plans to go out. No boyfriend to make plans with. Just that morning she'd questioned if she was even capable of love.

How can a thirty-year-old, modern, successful woman not have a man?

Jordan, her other best friend, had invited her a few days ago to the grand opening of the new scuba shop her boyfriend Zac and his business partner were opening that weekend. *Mar Profundo USA* would be the best new dive shop in town.

Liddy wouldn't miss it. But it wouldn't be as enjoyable flying solo, especially now that her friends had significant others.

Shit! She needed to break out of this gloomy funk.

When the hell was their next vacation? For the past two years, she and her besties escaped the daily grind on a week-long vacation, usually someplace warm and sunny. Both times, Sam and Jordan each found love.

Liddy'd found a beach snow globe. On their last trip to Puerto Vallarta, she'd spotted the little trinket in the Malecon market, and had to get it—snow over a sandy beach in *Mexico*.

Ironic.

"Ha," she said to the empty space, staring at the snow globe on the windowsill over her kitchen sink.

After years of being a love addict with all the wrong men,

Liddy now felt that love was overrated.

Maybe I should get a cat.

She gripped the edge of the stainless-steel sink. *Oh God, did I just think that?*

Liddy moved to the living room, where her record player rested on a bookshelf. Feathering through the stacks of LP's beside it always made her smile and brought her back to when she'd first come to her parents' home as their foster child, eventually, their adopted daughter. She'd instantly fallen in love with the machine so when her mom offered it as a housewarming gift, she didn't hesitate to accept.

She put on an old Steely Dan record, and tried to let the music soothe her.

This place was all hers. She adored her little home put together by yard-sale treasures and hand-me-downs acquired over the years. A sofa from her parents' house, a coffee table from Sam, and an old armoire she'd picked up from a flea market and refinished herself. Sparsely decorated, but she was never one for material things. She'd chosen each piece for functionality and the timeless style.

All things she managed on a modest salary plus commission, but living in San Francisco, she had to be frugal with all her other purchases.

Despite the pride in putting together a nice home in the most expensive city in the country, she needed a change of scenery.

Two weeks until Thanksgiving, and the last thing she felt

was *thankful.* Maybe that change in scenery would help put her in a festive spirit. Her boss had suggested she take some vacation before the holiday season got too crazy.

She turned on the stove to heat water for tea.

That was the answer. Their last vacation had been over a year and half ago. Time to get the heck out of town—and nowhere *near* Mexico.

She stopped the record player, and reached for her phone. "Jordan."

"Hey, *chica.* What's up?" The sound of creaking trampolines and pounding vaults thundered in the background. She glanced at the time on her phone. The gymnastics coach should be finished with her high school team practice by now.

"J, sorry. I thought practice would be over."

"It's okay. We're wrapping up."

"So, what's the chance, after opening weekend for the dive shop, you, me, and Sam can go on vacation?"

"Um, pretty good for me. School's out the whole week of Thanksgiving. Does that work?"

"Hell, yes. I'm sick and tired of the rain. Ya know what else?"

"I know, you're sick and tired of being sick and tired."

"Damn straight." They chuckled together.

"Okay, I'll do some digging. How do you feel about snow skiing?" Jordan asked.

She bit her lip. "I would love to, but that's a bit out of my price range. Hotel *and* lift passes..."

"Oh, don't worry about that. Zac's cousin works at a ski resort in Colorado, and can get us lift tickets. Which is why I thought of it."

"Fabulous! I'll call Sam."

She disconnected the line and punched Sam's preset button. Liddy's heart rate increased with excitement.

"Samantha Louise Callahan, soon to be Bradshaw," she announced when Sam picked up.

"Lydia Michelle Drake," her friend countered playfully.

"I need a vacation."

"Oh, God. Me too. This wedding stuff is making me cross-eyed."

"Jordan's looking into a ski trip. You up for it?"

"Long overdue. I'm in!"

"Super. I'll let you know when I hear from J."

Liddy set down her phone and poured the hot water over her tea bag. Suddenly, she could breathe a little easier. The rain lashing at her window didn't matter as much anymore either. She was leaving town.

Oh yeah.

Chapter TWO

JORDAN, YOU HAVE totally outdone yourself," Liddy exclaimed.

The ladies walked through the doorway of their private cabin at Buffalo Ridge Ski Lodge in the Colorado Mountains, and Liddy couldn't believe her eyes. A spacious living area with a huge stone fireplace, already stocked with wood, adjacent to a modern kitchen, and real hardwood flooring throughout. Looking up, Liddy spied heavy wood beams, modern track lighting, and a ceiling fan. To the side, a door led to the bedroom with two queen beds and en suite bathroom.

Jordan tipped the young bellhop who had so kindly showed them to their woodsy home for the next several days. He pointed out the easiest way to get to the ski lift, and ran through all the amenities, which were mostly housed at the Lodge.

Liddy pulled her rolling suitcase into the bedroom. The same red and black buffalo-check curtains hung over the windows as were in the living room, and the TV sat in a dark-stained oak armoire. With as tiny as her budget was, she was stunned their funds stretched this far—thanks to some helpful connections.

She heaved her luggage onto the bed, only to have the mattress split in the middle. The small gap revealed they'd shoved two twin beds together to make it a queen-sized bed.

"I know we're super close and have had to spoon each other in the same bed on other trips, but do you mind if I split this sucker into two?"

"Sweet," Sam laughed. "I'll try not to be too disappointed."

Liddy strolled into the bathroom and gasped.

"What is it?" Sam passed through the door. "Holy crap!"

"This is insane," she breathed.

They both stared at the oversized bathroom, complete with a marble-top, double-sink vanity, stand-up shower, and large white air-jet tub. It practically begged Liddy to dive in.

"Cool, huh?" Jordan asked from over their shoulders. "That'll be good for soaking after a long day on the slopes."

"But before margaritas," Sam chimed in.

"Exactly." Jordan grinned, then turned to the bedroom to unpack her luggage. "Hey, girls."

Sam and Liddy spun around, looking at Jordan from the doorway. "We know. We know. We have ten minutes to get into our swimsuits," Liddy said.

Jordan peered up and then laughed. "Now, that would

be a sight. I was gonna say let's go back to the Lodge, check out the place, and get our skis rented before the shop closes."

"Great idea." Sam opened her luggage. "Then we'll grab dinner at the restaurant and maybe a few drinks."

"I'm so excited," Liddy said. "I have a good feeling about this vacation. Fresh, crisp air, fire in the fireplace, and as much skiing as we can fit in a day."

"Amen," said Sam.

"And after Puerto Vallarta, you deserve to have an extra good time," Jordan declared.

"You know it, sista."

THE LODGE BUSTLED with guests—some with ski equipment, some with luggage, and a few warming up by the oversized stone fireplace. The grand space held caramel leather couches and club chairs on fluffy white rugs across the hardwood floor. The coffee bar on the far side filled the whole room with a delicious dark coffee bean scent, with hints of cinnamon. A moose head and deer head stared at each other from opposite ends of the room, leading up to the vaulted ceilings with several chandeliers made of antlers.

A tall, unfairly handsome man stood with a group of people gathered around him—cutting up and laughing—everyone's eyes glued to him.

The ladies headed for the front desk, and were greeted by a thin man with light brown hair. His name tag read

"Russell."

"What can I help you with, ladies?"

"We need a map of the lifts and runs. Also, could you tell us where the ski shop is?" Jordan asked.

Russell slid two maps and a list of activities across the counter. The young man's eyes twinkled, and when he smiled his perfect white teeth looked too big for his mouth.

"Here we are." He circled a spot on the map. "Here's the lift to take you farther up the mountain to the central ski resort where you'll find the lifts leading to all the runs."

"Cool," she replied.

"There's also a restaurant if you want to break for lunch."

"Great. Out of curiosity, who is that gentleman over there?" Jordan discreetly pointed to the jester in dark pants and a long-sleeved forest-green shirt with a buffalo on the breast.

"Oh." Russell's eyes lit up. "That's Luke Sawyer. He's our lead ski instructor. Best in the county. Isn't he cute? If you ladies need lessons, *he's* the one you want. Talented, and delicious eye candy, too." He winked.

"Okay, thanks." Jordan chuckled. She walked away from the counter, and pulled Sam and Liddy in close.

"No better compliment," Sam whispered, "than a gay man's recommendation."

"Girls, I think we need ski lessons, don't you?" Jordan's smile stretched from ear to ear.

Sam grinned.

Liddy glanced Luke's way as he let out a boisterous laugh that could probably be heard at the next resort over. "Nah. I'm good." She knew what her friends were doing, but that man was not her type. "He's a little loud, and seems a bit self-centered." Even as the words came out, the semi-circle of people around him grew.

Oh brother. She knew the kind—egomaniac who thought he was God's gift to women and was only satisfied when every single eye in the room was glued on his ass.

"Are you sure?" Sam asked, lifting a brow. "Because he sure is cute."

"If I wasn't with Zac," Jordan piped up, "I'd go after that tall drink of water myself."

She wrinkled her nose. "Pass. Let's go get our skis, okay?"

Jordan watched her face. "Are you serious? Look how playful he is with everyone. He's perfect for you."

"How 'bout I take it easy on this trip with the men? I still haven't recovered from last time."

Liddy'd been drugged *and* robbed.

Damn, she needed a good man, but her attempts at finding a romantic fling the last time were near disastrous. Come to think of it, in the past year and a half, her casual dates lacked luster since her heart wasn't in it. Likely, because she didn't trust herself anymore.

So, definitely no men this trip.

"If you say so," Jordan said, doubt lacing her voice.

LIDDY TREKKED DOWN the path alone toward the Lodge just before twilight. *Shit!* After she'd unpacked, she'd found her goggles had cracked in her luggage during flight. She had no choice but to buy a pair from the shop for the duration of the vacation. While spending the money irritated her beyond belief, it was either that or go without.

Flurries of snow danced in the air, and Liddy stopped among the pine trees and breathed in the fresh air. Crisp and refreshing. Just perfect. It had been far too long since her last winter vacation. Her favorite, even more so than beach trips.

Shortly after her parents had adopted her, they'd brought her skiing to Lake Tahoe, to celebrate. That trip had triggered her love for snow skiing though the last time had been with her parents as a college graduation present, where they'd secretly saved to surprise her by returning to Lake Tahoe in celebration.

Between working at the boutique and volunteering at Holly House, there was hardly any time for socializing. Damn, life had been crazy lately. Well, the entirety of her life had been crazy, actually. Thank God she had two of the best friends a woman could ask for to keep her in check. To remind her that she was, indeed, not psychotic, and more than worthy of the best kind of relationship.

The Lodge sat before her like a long, log cabin, an oasis in a desert of heavenly, frozen wonderland. The warm light in the windows gave it a Candyland cottage appeal in a frosting landscape.

She smiled.

A few steps into the Lodge, and Liddy had to catch her breath. It would take a while to get used to the altitude. The lobby was even more packed than when they'd first arrived. The rental shop was toward the back, and she wound her way through the throng of people.

The same handsome and loud man from earlier that day now stood by the back door, calling people out.

"Anyone need skiing lessons? We have the best instructors on the planet, right here at Buffalo Ridge. Or at least the best ones who showed up to their final exams." He grinned and got a few chuckles from bystanders. "We promise full support and positive reinforcement, and will only make fun of you behind your back. We encourage everyone to take a nice full shot of whiskey before they put on their skis, to help loosen up your muscles and your wallets for extra tips."

"Oh, brother," Liddy mumbled under her breath, and pushed through a crowd of teenagers watching the man's pathetic excuse for a sales pitch.

The instructor continued, "Safety is our top priority, followed closely by leaving all inhibitions at the door."

Just as I expected—one of those guys.

Liddy had almost made it to the end of the hallway.

"You, the gorgeous woman in the white coat trying to sneak by..."

Liddy froze. And cringed.

The man grinned. "You look like you could use ski lessons. Or at least a stiff drink at the bar."

She straightened her spine, and addressed him eye-to-eye, despite all the gawkers and bystanders. "Are you the instructor? *My* instructor?"

"I can be, for you."

Liddy smiled. "Then, no thanks."

The man's smile slipped. A few guests oohed at the burn, and others chuckled.

"Why not?" he asked.

Never mind that I ski black diamonds, I just don't like you. "If it were with one of the others, I might consider it."

A few more hisses came from the crowd.

She turned to find the rental shop, but she heard his footsteps behind her, trying to follow.

"Wait, you don't like me? Everyone likes me."

"I can't imagine why," Liddy threw over her shoulder.

He laughed, the sound of his voice much closer than before. "Why don't you like me?"

"You're obnoxious. *And* I already know how to ski."

"I could make you better."

She rolled her eyes. "Modesty is so hard to find these days."

"I'm not being cocky, just trying to find the best way to talk to you more. It's not every day an angel walks into Buffalo Ridge."

Liddy whirled, and glared at him head on. *An angel.*

That's what the jackass in Mexico had called her, right before he'd dropped a roofie in her drink and stole her stuff. Now, she never trusted it. "I'm not interested."

He raised his hands in surrender, and chuckled. "Okay, fair enough. I'll see you on the slopes. Be safe."

As he walked away, she picked up a pair of stylish purple goggles.

Arrogant asswipe.

Chapter THREE

LUKE BREATHED IN the fresh mountain air the next morning. A light dusting coated the trees all around the resort, and a thin layer of clouds haloed the mountain ridge. Sunlight gleamed through like heaven smiling down on his favorite place in the world.

He greeted his students as they slowly filtered to the meeting spot from the resort below. His two fellow instructors, Jason and Patrick, had ridden up to the mountain resort earlier to get everything together. For a holiday week, it would be busy.

Dazzling blonde hair cascading down a white jacket caught his attention, and his heart skipped.

Liddy.

He'd learned the name of that little fireball last night after she'd rebuffed him, and couldn't wait to see her again. After their interaction the day before, he was a goner. With the exception of his family, no one talked to him like that. Maybe it was the challenge or that smart mouth attached to that gorgeous body, but he had to get to know her.

He turned to Jason and Patrick. "Hold the fort for a second."

He approached her and her friends while they stood in line waiting for the lifts to open.

"Last chance, I've got an opening for lessons, Liddy."

Her eyes narrowed. "How do you know my name?"

"I have an inside source."

"Hi. I'm Jordan," the brunette said with an adorable smile. "This is Sam."

"Nice to meet you, ladies. I'm Luke Sawyer, the resort's ski instructor." He stepped closer, the sun bouncing off her blonde hair to make it nearly platinum. He wondered what her perfume was like, if she was the flowery, sweet kind, or the spicy, more flavorful kind. Out here in the packed snow and cold breeze, it was impossible to determine. "Here." He held out his hand to Liddy, like he had something in his palm. "Hold this for me for a second, would you?"

Either on instinct, or just being polite, she complied, looking at him funny.

Which is exactly what he wanted. He slipped his fingers between hers, and squeezed, then brought her knuckles up, and pulled her in closer.

Her shocked face was priceless. Wide, beautiful, deep hazel eyes that pierced his soul. Parted, pink lips that just ached to be kissed.

"I've been wanting to do that ever since I saw you."

She scowled, and yanked her hand away.

He laughed. "Just trying to loosen you up. You can't take life too seriously up here."

"Is that a resort rule," she spat, "or is that one of your specialty—bumper-sticker anecdotes?" She stepped back toward her friends, clearly unamused.

"Just a hobby. My specialty is far more specific." He flashed her a grin.

To which she scowled further.

"Sorry," he chuckled. He glanced at the other two ladies. "Just trying to convince your friend here to let me show her a few things."

Jordan and Sam giggled. "Yeah, she can be a tough nut to crack sometimes," Jordan said.

"A real tigress," Sam chimed in.

"Well, let me know if you change your mind." He looked at Liddy, drinking in those gorgeous hazel eyes.

"Uh-huh."

He spun around to head back to the meeting spot and could have sworn he heard Liddy say, *You two are gonna pay.* He grinned.

Oh yeah. A little firecracker, that one.

He freakin' loved it.

LIDDY HAD MADE it nearly to the bottom, her lungs full of refreshing mountain air for the last two hours. Sam and

Jordan lagged behind a ways, and she'd really wanted a little time to herself this run. She pulled over to the side to adjust her ski boot, which had started to feel loose. After resecuring the footing and snapping it back in, she noticed a sign pointing to Sparks Pond. Along a path through the tall pine trees about fifty yards in, light glinted off what looked like frosted glass on the ground.

She slid over uneven snow until she came upon the frozen water.

A small pond the size of an Olympic swimming pool gleamed in the broken rays of sunshine through the pine trees. The water was frozen through, with a dark gloss on the surface. On the other side were a few benches and picnic tables covered in snow. Clearly, a camping ground during the summer months.

"Wow," Liddy breathed.

The tree branches cracked in the breeze, swaying to their own rhythm of the world. A hidden gem in the frozen jungle of Colorado.

She'd bet a number of romantic trysts took place here at night, as well.

But not for her. Another boyfriend to reject her? No, thank you. She could enjoy magical places like this enough in solitude.

Laughs from skiers back on the run rang in the air. The girls would be waiting for her at the bottom. She turned around, albeit a little awkwardly, and slid back through the trees. Once on the run, she checked to make sure the path was clear, and pushed forward.

Picking up speed, she was just in her groove when a snowboarder zoomed in front of her.

"On your right," he barked too late.

Liddy struggled to swerve out his way. She leaned on her skis, twisting away.

The ski didn't move with her.

Her body fell to the side, and something popped in her ankle.

She screamed through the pain, and tried to catch herself, but that didn't stop her momentum.

Liddy landed hard on her shoulder. The padding on her coat helped to keep it from hurting too much. The searing burn in her ankle intensified. She shifted to her butt just as she'd learned years ago, and let gravity take her down the run on her back until her uncontrollable slide eventually stopped.

The sky pulsed over her head. Crystal blue with snowflakes fluttering around her, the beauty mocked her pain. Her face burned, and the few flakes that landed on her cheeks only offered slight relief.

"Ow," she groaned to the clouds. Her whole body screamed. She looked down to see her hands still gripping the poles—one metal shaft bent in half, the other stuck into the snow by her thigh. Only one foot was attached to a ski. The other ski was missing.

"Don't move!" someone shouted behind her.

Wasn't gonna.

The crunching sound of skis over snow drew closer. Then someone snapping out of their skis and running over in footsteps, not nearly as loud as her panting.

A face interrupted her view of the sky.

Wide, sapphire eyes and red cheeks. A soft mouth, smooth enough to kiss. That was her first thought. Until the features coalesced, coming together into Luke—the arrogant ski instructor.

She scowled. "I'm fine."

He moved her poles and stepped closer. "Can you sit up?"

"Of course, I can." She struggled with the idea, then forced herself to try.

His arm wrapped around her back, helping her. "Easy."

"I got it."

Her hat fell off as her body protested against the motion. Frigid air invaded her scalp.

"I saw what happened," Luke continued. "Your efforts to stay upright deserve a nine and a half, at least. If it weren't for that shoddy landing."

His smile was just as annoying as his insult.

"Go away," she shoved his arm off, only for the vicious pain in her ankle to shoot up her leg. She grabbed for it, making the pain worse.

"That's what you get for attempting violence," he chuckled, then spoke into the radio on his shoulder. "Sawyer to Lodge. We need Ski Patrol on Bluemoon, just below Sparks Pond. Injured skier."

"Copy that. ETA five minutes," the radio crackled.

"You're lucky we're toward the bottom of the run. Can you wiggle your toes?"

She moved them as best she could; it was hard to tell through the throbbing. "I think so."

"Good. Because you didn't scream bloody murder, it's unlikely that you broke anything. That said, I'll leave your boot on until they can get pain meds in you."

"What are you, a doctor?"

"Nope, been doing this a long time. You know, if you wanted to be alone with me, you could've just asked. Not gone to all this effort," he said with a cocky grin.

Liddy glared. "You're really in love with yourself, aren't you?"

"You're the first who isn't. Everyone loves me. What's wrong with *you*?"

The urge to slap him was very strong. "Not a damn thing."

"All evidence to the contrary." He motioned to her ankle. "Sit back and let the professionals handle this."

"I'm not letting you handle *anything* on me."

"That is such a shame—because this beauty needs ice. Right away."

The ski patrol arrived, and not a moment too soon. They asked her a ton of questions, like her name, what happened, could she move her toes, where was her pain level on a scale of one to ten.

Ten. It was a damn ten. Dr. Luke Sawyer thought it wasn't broken, but she wasn't so sure. It was all she could do to hold back the tears. How she wished her friends were near.

"Can you call Sam and Jordan?"

"Sure," Luke replied although she'd directed the question to the ski patrol. She gave both her friend's cell phone numbers. Hopefully they could meet her at the clinic.

They shot some pain reliever up her nose, which started working within seconds. As they held her right leg steady, she hoisted herself onto the gurney using her left leg and arms.

"We got it from here, Luke."

"It's okay, I'll go down with you guys." Luke lifted his skis and walked alongside the gurney. Occasionally, he asked, "Doing okay?"

She was in too much pain to respond beyond a thumbs up.

Slowly, they trailed down the run, finally making it to the clinic. Once on the table, people bustled about giving her nasal cannula for oxygen and an IV of pain meds, so they could remove the boot to investigate further.

Alex, the lead, couldn't be much older than Liddy, and would be super cute if it wasn't for his crooked nose. Poor guy probably broke it snow-boarding and it never healed properly. "Okay, Liddy, what do you think your pain level is at now?"

"About a three."

"Great. We're going to take your boot off now."

"Well, crap. Okay, let's do it." She closed her eyes and tried a few deeps breaths.

Alex, Luke, and another guy carefully pulled the boot off and Liddy barely cried out. That could be a good sign. Alex gently pulled away her sock, and touched several areas, checking for breaks and tenderness.

After a few minutes, he said, "Doesn't appear broken. I think you sprained it. The doctor will take an x-ray to make sure when you get down off the mountain."

Fan-fucking-tastic. There goes my whole vacation.

At that moment, Sam and Jordan walked through the clinic's door.

"Ohmigosh. What the hell happened?" Jordan started. Sam held Liddy's hand.

"They think I sprained my ankle."

Jordan looked over at Alex. "So, what does that mean?"

"If that's the case, she needs to be off of it for three days. But it would be best to talk to the doc."

"Okay, let's go," Jordan said.

"How exactly are we going to do that? We took the lift," Sam asked with eyebrows raised.

"My car is up here," Luke replied. "John, bring that wheelchair over, would you? Let's get you loaded in, then we can transfer you to my car."

Luke effortlessly lifted her off the exam table, like she weighed no more than a pillow. His woodsy aftershave reminded her of sitting by a warm campfire. He gently placed her in the wheelchair.

"Is that okay?" he asked, his tender stare more sincere than she'd expected.

Her tongue tied up, and all she could do was nod.

Liddy had to admit, for an egocentric, loudmouth Romeo, Luke seemed to be rather congenial.

After loading the ski gear in the back of Luke's SUV, they all piled into the car, Liddy in the backseat, propping her foot on the leather, careful not to jostle her leg.

Luke called the doctor on the slow drive to the resort, telling him about her injury.

After x-rays and several minutes with the doctor, who reminded Liddy of Ross from *Friends*, he confirmed what Alex said earlier. No breaks, but a third-degree sprain. She'd have to keep it elevated, ice it, and stay off it for three days.

Shit!

Every single trip, there is always something to ruin it. This might very well be the last vacation she ever took.

Jordan and Sam hung close while the doctor dug out some pain medicine.

"You okay?" Sam asked.

"This sucks. I'm a curse."

"Girl, I am so sorry," Jordan said with a frown. "Don't you ever say that about yourself."

"Three days puts us at Wednesday night," Liddy thought out loud. "We're supposed to leave Thursday to make it back for turkey dinner. You see where I'm going with this?"

"I know. So, why don't I see if we can stay an extra day?" Jordan asked, clasping her free hand. "Then we can at least have Thursday to ski. I'll look into it."

Well, that was something. She'd miss her family on Thanksgiving, but she'd miss skiing a hell of a lot more. Frankly, if this was her last ski trip for eternity, she'd like to enjoy what she could.

I'm either a curse, or have the worst luck on the planet!

Chapter FOUR

LIDDY HAD THE two bestest girlfriends in the world.

Jordan went to the gift shop for a bunch of goodies while Sam made her lunch for later.

"I have magazines, crosswords, and look at this cutie," Jordan said as she held up a paperback with a handsome man on the cover and "Prince" in the title. "If I can't give you the real thing, maybe I can at least give you a book boyfriend."

Liddy giggled.

Sam stepped away from the kitchen. "Okay, babe. In the fridge is a turkey sandwich, cottage cheese, and pickles." Then she pointed to the counter. "I set out chips and a can of soup. You won't be able to carry the bowl, but I think you can reach from the stove to the counter and eat here."

Liddy eyed the distance and Sam was right. "You guys thought of everything."

Jordan rubbed her back. "You sure you're going to be alright?"

"Yes."

"Need anything else?" Sam asked.

Liddy shook her head. "Actually, can you take my skis back in the morning? Since I won't be using them until Thursday, give me a chance to save a few bucks."

Her friend frowned. "I'm so sorry. This whole trip has been ruined. Are you sure you don't want to just go home?"

"Absolutely not! You guys are having a blast. No way in hell am I going to take you away from it." *And this is still a break from dreary home.*

They each pecked her on the head and made their way into the snowy winter wonderland.

WITH JORDAN AND Sam on the slopes, Liddy was determined to enjoy the private time in a nice hot bath. She knew for a fact the resort had stocked bubble bath for guests to relish that ginormous air-jet tub.

"Finally. At least one good thing about the vacation," she told nobody.

She hobbled on her crutches to the bathroom and blasted the water to fill the tub. Fishing for the bubble bath, she selected a crème brûlée honey scent and poured the entire sampler in the water.

Better than any spa. "Now we're talkin'."

She fully intended on bringing that sexy romance book into the bath with her, and escaping to a royal book boyfriend's bedroom, at least in her imagination.

The model on the cover was certainly handsome—exotic,

scruffy face with a pristine tuxedo. An image of the arrogant ski instructor entered her mind unbidden. No, she wanted a luxurious, relaxing bath, not a reminder of that loud-mouthed man. She forced the picture from her mind.

She maneuvered back to the bed to sit and strip. Staying off her foot for three days was certainly no picnic, but Liddy was determined to heal completely. She'd always been a good patient, convinced the more strict one followed the rules, the faster one healed. If only she'd been that way in her relationships.

After she managed to get everything off, her reflection moved in the mirror above the dresser. Even from several feet away, the white scar at her clavicle was clear. A permanent reminder of where she'd come from. Her first foster family when she was six years old, where the father had beat her with the plastic doll she'd always carried around until he'd broken it on her body.

No need to relive that moment. I'm so much stronger now.

The click of the door pulled her from the memory.

"Liddy," an unmistakably *male* voice called out. "I have ice."

Luke!

She froze.

Shit! There she stood by the side of the bed, stark naked, and Luke had just entered the cabin.

She dropped the crutches and belly-flopped across the

bed, yanking the covers over her. Her heart hammered in her chest like a racehorse.

"There you are. How come your leg isn't up?"

She lifted her head to see him standing at her feet, hands on his hips. "Um, I wanted to take a bath."

He glanced at the open bathroom door, where the water was still going. "How's that working for ya', since you're still in bed?" His head tipped to the side and his eyebrows lifted. "There's no slacking in rehab."

Before she could respond, he whipped the covers off, exposing the backside of her completely naked body.

She shrieked.

"Time to . . . Oh, holy hell!"

"Luke!" She reached for the covers, but she wasn't fast enough.

He pulled them away, dangling just out of her reach. "Oh, no you don't. That has to be the fucking most gorgeous ass I've ever seen in my life. I'm getting my fill."

"Luke! You asshole! Don't you even knock?!"

He raised the sheet. When she grabbed it, he didn't let go. Instead, he stepped forward, knelt one knee beside her thighs, and leaned down over her back until his lips were mere inches from her ear. "Knock? If you want, I'll knock you screaming and panting into next week."

Oh crap! Her spine tingled instantly. Why did that sound so damn good? Why did she even like the thought of being with this . . . this crude-mouthed egomaniac?

Damn!

"Now, get that insanely fuckable ass in the tub and make it quick. You've got thirty minutes. When I come back, if you're not done, I'm biting that ass, and you won't want to sit down for a week."

He stood, and as she reached for the covers . . .

Slap!

"Ouch!" He'd slapped her bare bottom, like she was three. How dare he!

"Thirty minutes, sweet cheeks."

His footfalls moved away, and the door slammed shut.

"Ohmigod," she breathed out. "What the hell just happened?"

She lay on the bed another minute, assessing the rush of emotion. Her ass cheek burned where he'd slapped her, and her spine still hadn't stopped tingling. His antics had created a pool of moisture between her legs.

No, this can't be right, she thought to herself. *I'm not that kinda girl.*

She sucked in a breath. Twenty-nine minutes left.

She twisted into a sitting position, grabbed the crutches off the floor, and shuffled into the bathroom to her awaiting pool of heaven.

The romance novel sat on the bathroom counter. Liddy ignored it. There was more than enough heat in that bathroom already.

Sinking into the water, all she could think was *who the*

hell does he think he is? That, and *how do I get more of it?*

LUKE CLOSED THE door behind him, and let out a deep exhale.

What the fuck was that?

He absolutely had no right to do those things, make those moves on Liddy. She was a guest at the resort! She could get him fired.

That little pistol got the best of him. She was spit and fire for sure, and he had the fucking hardest time staying away from her. But damn if that wildcat didn't surprise him. Pulling back the covers, he'd thought he was getting her butt in gear. He had no earthly idea he'd find that gorgeous ass attached to that gorgeous naked body sprawled out before him.

The better man would have A, not touched the covers in the first place, and B, quickly recovered her and apologized immediately for crossing the line.

But no. A switch flipped in Luke that even *he* didn't recognize. He had to see that beautiful body in person, revel in it, appreciate it, like it was meant to be appreciated. Truth be told, at that moment, he'd give his company stock to see the entire package.

Now, he'd worked himself into a corner. He'd told her he'd be back in thirty minutes or there'd be hell to pay. But he couldn't walk back in there. His dick raged in his jeans, and seeing her again wouldn't be wise. He'd lose his self-control all over again.

He headed to his room straight away and called the Lodge for assistance. Rebecca picked up.

"Hey, Becca."

"Hey, Luke."

"Listen, I'm supposed to check on Liddy in Cabin Eight in twenty minutes. Make sure she has water, and fresh ice for her sprain. Something's come up I need to handle. Would you mind dropping in on her for me?"

"Sure, no problem."

"Great. I appreciate it."

He disconnected the call and dropped the phone on his bed. Then, without giving it another thought, he stripped naked, entered his en suite bathroom, and blasted the water for a cold shower.

Working that little wench out of his system wouldn't be easy. There was a definite possibility she'd be downright impossible to stay clear of.

He groaned under the spray.

He was a professional and needed to start acting like one. Never before had a resort guest ever gotten under his skin like Liddy.

Chapter

FIVE

LUKE SQUEEZED THE foam buffalo with the resort logo, a marketing stress toy, as he swirled around in the chair in his office. He still couldn't get that woman out of his mind.

His phone vibrated along the desk. He glanced at the caller ID. *Mom.*

He stared at it, letting it dance across his roster list for several more rings. He wanted to talk to her. He really did. It was Thanksgiving week, for heaven's sake. What normal man wouldn't at least *talk* to his family over the holidays?

Since when has my family ever been normal?

He gave the stress buffalo another squeeze, and answered.

"Hey, Mom." He leaned back in the executive chair, the leather worn and comfortable.

"I have Jerome on standby to come get you if you'd like." His mother's smooth, musical voice made him smile, the same way it had when he was a child. One of her many gifts that made it so easy for people to fall in love with her, particularly his father, was that she made everyone feel at ease, welcome, and appreciated, as if they were the only one in the room.

"Then you should probably let Jerome have the week off, so he can spend it with his family. I'm staying out here this week."

The sigh on the other end was also the exact same. "We hardly get to see you anymore, darling."

"I just saw you all for Chloe's birthday bash."

"That was *May*. Six months ago. Do you honestly hate us that much that you refuse to spend time with us?"

Always the dramatics. But Luke wouldn't fall for it. There was a plan behind everything his mother said. He glanced out the open door, making sure no one passed by. "I love spending time with you. When you aren't talking business, legacy, or chastising me for my chosen profession."

"We don't *always* discuss business. It's just your father's way of trying to entice you to come home. Make you feel included and up to date when you decide to come back, instead of being a recluse in the mountains."

He snorted.

There are so many things wrong in her statement.

"Just because I don't want to be in the mix of Manhattan tycoons does not mean I'm a recluse. I'm hardly ever alone up here. More importantly, when are you going to hear me? *This* is my home."

"I still don't understand why you're out there."

Here we go.

"I honestly thought your sojourn to the mountains was just a temporary thing because of Ashley. In ten years, you're still not over her?"

Luke ground his teeth together. "I think a decade on this mountain proves it's more than that."

"Do you have any idea what you could do with your business degree here? Your father has a position all lined up for you."

His patience wore thin, and his blood pressure rocketed. He put down the buffalo before he ripped holes in it. "I'm using my education well enough. This is *my* life, Mother. This is what I want. We've gone over this *ad nauseum*. I'm not interested in boring corporate America."

"Luke," his mom's voice softened. "I'm sorry our life in society is such a disappointment to you. But all the *boring corporate America* mentality you so look down on has made our family what it is. It's given you all your experiences to get you where you are. And I've made my life about charity and giving back. What's so wrong with that?"

"Absolutely nothing." His mother rarely poured the guilt trip, but when she did, it was prime real estate. "Because it makes you happy and fulfilled. Right?"

"Of course. There's responsibility with this life. I take it seriously."

"Same here—I have responsibilities with my job that I take seriously, too. *That life*, yours and Dad's, is not fulfilling to me. I'm not saying I'm superior, it's just not for me. I appreciate *everything* you both have done, but this is my choice."

Her deep sigh on the other end was shaky and he recognized tears behind it.

He hated hearing her cry.

"Mom, I've already booked my flight for Christmas. I'll be out there through New Year's, so I'll see you all very soon."

"Don't be silly," she replied, the shake in her voice dissipating. "We'll send—"

"Jerome, I know. But I'd rather fly commercial."

His mother groaned. "Says no sane person in this country."

"I've never claimed sanity." He chuckled.

"I love you, sweet boy."

He smiled. That warm voice would always make him smile. "I love you, too. Give everyone a hug for me."

"You'll do that yourself at Christmas."

He ended the call and stared at the painting on the far end of the room. Snow-capped mountains scraping the heavens at sunrise, with a small bonfire in the valley below. He could just feel the fresh, frigid air in the painting against his face.

His mother *had* to bring up that name again. *Ashley.*

Luke scowled.

The tea light in the mini hurricane vase flickered as Luke's father finished his toast. Eloquent words about the next generation, continuing the family legacy, and the empires of America.

The five-star meal he'd just finished churned in his stomach. He ignored it. Instead, he focused on the leather portfolio in front of him. The one he'd received only hours before that contained his degree certificate. His father already had the plaque ordered in the mail.

"To Luke," his father boomed at the front of the room. A large room with a dozen tables, all full with family, friends, and business colleagues. Every seat taken at this prestigious event—the graduation of a Rothchild.

Ashley held up her champagne glass, and rubbed his arm. Her smile so beautiful, her eyes glittering from the candlelight.

Everyone in the room stood, and held out their flutes. Staring at him. Smiling at him. Full of expectations. Most of them assumed he was a carbon-copy of his father, both in appearance and ambition. The youngest Rothchild son.

He grabbed his champagne and toasted back to his father. He knew his place. He knew every social protocol and just how to behave amongst the captains of industry all gathered in the room. He forced air into his lungs, hoping the stifling atmosphere was just the rumbling food in his gut.

Toasts finished, and the waiters served the desserts, chocolate soufflés, creme brulees and raspberry joconde cake. His mother's favorite.

Ashley kissed him on the cheek, her sweet perfume

doing nothing for his nausea. "I'll be right back. Just going to freshen up."

He stood, then pulled out her seat to escort her to the back of the room.

Her glittery sapphire dress swayed as she walked, her figure well defined. Definitely her signature color with her platinum blonde hair pulled back into an elegant French twist. Her neck lasted for days in that style. He'd spent many nights nuzzling and kissing her creamy skin.

She escaped to the bathroom, blowing him a kiss when she turned the corner.

He stood back, and several more women followed.

The things that took place in the women's restroom every man had always wondered.

He grabbed another champagne flute from a passing waiter.

"Son." His father emerged from the crowd like the parting seas, eyes on him from every angle. Which meant those eyes were on Luke, too.

He held out his hand, and Luke shook it. His father pulled him into a tight hug. "I'm so proud of you. The next stage in your life begins. The next era of Rothchild."

Luke swallowed back a bitter taste rising in his throat. "We should talk later tonight."

His father's grin widened. "Absolutely. There's much to discuss. Including..." he looked around him, careful to lower his voice. "An engagement, I hear? Ashley's a fine choice.

Elite stock."

"That hasn't been decided," Luke murmured low.

"No? Well, son, you should figure that out fairly quickly. It's all the mothers can talk about."

He fixed his suit coat, not quite ready for that discussion. He loved Ashley, and had no doubts her family would approve of him. But he needed to be sure of something first.

"Are you all right? You look a little off."

He forced a confident smile. "I'll be right back. Too much dessert."

He moved through the ballroom lobby, careful to keep his practiced confidence in his walk to the bathroom. A Rothchild could never display weakness in public, and always kept his cool.

Just before he reached the hallway with the restrooms, he recognized Ashley's voice from around the corner. Chatting with another woman. Likely her best friend, Sonya.

"I thought you said he'd pop the question tonight," her friend stated bluntly.

Luke stood behind the wall, careful to stay out of sight.

"It's still early," Ashley replied. She popped her lips together, like she was reapplying her lipstick.

"Actually, it's kinda late. You've been together what, four years, now?"

Ashley groaned. "I know. I'm exhausted. How many more jokes do I have to pretend to laugh at? Orgasms do I have to fake? His face used to be so charming, and now it's just..."

What the fuck? *A frigid shiver raced down his spine, like someone had poured liquid nitrogen over his back.*

"Once I land that ring, I won't have to try so hard. I'll be super busy with wedding plans, and I'll finally have my life set. Page six announcement, the whole world watching our nuptials like royalty—"

"Not to mention your own instant trust fund." Sonya's voice turned gleeful.

"The only thing that makes all of this worth it," Ashley replied, her voice lower. "Once I have that marriage certificate signed, I don't have to pretend to like him anymore."

Heat flooded his face. Nausea morphed to rage, then to instant anguish in a span of a heartbeat, then back to nausea.

He barreled into the men's room just in time for his dinner to come back up—heaving out his disbelief and fury. Thank God he was alone.

Alone. As if he didn't have enough on his plate . . . now this.

He had no idea how long it took to recover, but after splashing water on his face and getting the taste of vomit out of his mouth, he finally emerged back to the ballroom.

His father and mother stood at the entrance, waiting for him. Smiling at him, the whole room of American business waiting for him to join them.

Ashley stood beside his mother, her smile so gorgeous and outwardly genuine. Perfectly put together to portray the ideal trophy wife. Someone he'd thought he could share his life with. Who knew and appreciated him, not his family name, legacy, and wealth.

She'd so easily fooled him.

She held out her hand to join them.

Without a second glance, Luke turned and walked out.

He pinched the bridge of his nose. Branching out on his own was one of the best decisions he'd ever made. Nevertheless, it still stung like a sonuvabitch getting to this place.

But now was not the time to rehash the past—he had a blonde fireball to check on.

He scanned the office. If he was going to see that little pistol after their saucy interlude, maybe he should be prepared for payback. Did he have anything that would serve as protective armor?

Chapter SIX

THE HANDSOME PRINCE novel left Liddy hot and bothered on the couch in her tiny cabin of seclusion. She'd sailed through the story, along with half the crossword puzzles and three magazines Sam had bought her.

The clock glared back at her at just barely one in the afternoon—mocking her.

Outside the window, the sun peeked through the clouds, glittering off the snow path, which added extra misery to the mockery.

Her ankle ached up into her calf. The muscles needed to move. She grabbed the now-lukewarm ice bag from the couch, and staggered upright, using her crutches to hobble around the couch and into the kitchen. She pitched the water in the sink. The stocked fridge didn't entice her. She'd already had a sandwich for lunch an hour ago. The counters were spotless, so there was no need to clean.

She turned and spotted her ski gear next to the front door. Specifically, the goggles she'd bought at the shop. Which reminded her of the jackass, Luke, and the insane reaction she had to his slap.

She'd never felt so hot.

Heat flooded her cheeks at the memory.

"It's the damn boredom getting to you," she chided herself, dragging her hand down her face.

Liddy had never been one to laze around the house, even during her wallowing periods after breakups. She was always moving and on the go. Stuff to do, things to buy, and subsequently return when her frugal consciousness got the better of her.

Normally, in a post-breakup wallow, she'd get right back out there searching for a new prospect. Not the best of decisions, her friends would always remind her, but she couldn't help it. At least, not back then.

More of that pop-psychology, constantly seeking love that eluded her during childhood, and using one relationship after the next as a coping mechanism to deal with her fears of inadequacy.

Liddy was determined to stop that cycle.

Her confidence had improved greatly over the years, thanks to the unfailing support of her best friends.

But it was nearly impossible to feel confident in herself when she sat alone and helpless in the cabin, injured, and soaking in her own pity-party.

Her calf and ankle throbbed in sync and that annoyed the hell out of her.

"Come on, I haven't even been standing for three minutes."

She crutched back over to the couch, and set her foot on the ottoman. Reaching to massage the tendons was awkward, and only increased the throbbing.

Liddy leaned her head against the back of the couch, giving up the effort. Everything she tried hadn't helped.

She yanked the quilt over her legs, hoping a nap would make her feel better. Or at least distract her from the dreary day.

LUKE HAD LEARNED from the day before to knock on Liddy's door, but God as his witness, he wanted to see her beautiful, heart-shaped ass again. She was a vision—great body, smooth skin, and a helluva lot of grit.

"Come in," she called from the cabin.

"Are you sure? Or are you one of those women who lays around naked all the time?" he asked through the door. He opened the handle and stepped through. "As enticing as that would be, I could come back later."

Liddy lay on the sofa, legs up on the ottoman covered in a blanket, watching some game show. She wasn't smiling, clearly unamused by his joke.

Which meant she wasn't in the mood for his normal sense of humor. He decided to dial it way back. At least for now. "How are you doin' today?"

She glanced up, her mouth turned down into a pout. "What are you doing here? Don't you have a lesson or something?"

She wasn't trying to be nasty, but he knew he wasn't one of her favorite people. He wouldn't blame her, either. Maybe this was his chance to redeem himself. Or at least soften her up.

"In an hour, I do. Just checking in on you—saw your friends this morning and told them I would."

She nodded. "I'm okay. Occasionally, I get a weird ache or tingle," she scrunched up her adorable nose, "down my calf to my ankle."

"Hm, want me to take a look? I've seen enough of these injuries over the years."

"Yeah, okay."

He hiked up his jeans to comfortably crouch down at the end of the ottoman. He pulled back the blanket, revealing bare feet and legs.

Is she just wearing shorts with that tank top?

Surely, she'd want to wear fuzzy socks and flannel pants. "Aren't you cold?"

"Nah. This blanket keeps me warm."

The next thing he noticed—without surprise—was that her right ankle was still swollen. Third, the normal one was the most delicate ankle, and as his eyes wandered, he could see the shapeliness of her calves. He shouldn't think such things. He'd come to check up on her, make sure she was recovering—not to see her gorgeous bare body. Again.

Damn! His dick flexed in his jeans.

"When was the last time you iced it?"

"Um, about forty minutes ago."

"Okay, I'll get you fresh ice before I leave." He pressed along the top of her foot, working his way toward the talus, and gently up the tibia and fibula. "Does this hurt?"

"Not really."

"I can call the doctor to stop by and take a look at it, Liddy, but it's likely just part of the healing process."

She shook her head and glanced down quickly. "That's okay. I don't want to bother the doctor."

"If it worsens, we'll call him to examine it."

She murmured what might have been *okay*.

He rose and grabbed her refillable ice pouch. She had zero twinkle in her eyes; before, even when she'd chewed him out, there had been twinkle. She definitely seemed depressed but then again, missing out on the skiing and being cooped up in a small cabin couldn't be much fun.

He returned and set the ice pouch down beside the ottoman. "Here you go."

"Thanks," she mumbled.

He couldn't see for sure, but was she crying?

"Liddy, look at me."

She hesitated but gave him a quick glance. Tears clearly welled in her eyes.

He dropped to a knee beside her. "Liddy, what's wrong?

Are you hurt?"

She shook her head. "No, just having a little pity-party, I guess. I'm sad that this happened, but I'm also frustrated because I don't know what's going on with my ankle."

"Yeah, I get that." He couldn't help himself. He lifted his thumb to wipe away the stray tears that ran down her cheeks. He recalled on more than one occasion doing that for his sister back when her teenage heart had been broken. Nothing worse than seeing a woman cry.

And she didn't yell at him, which was a good sign.

"Would it help if I massage your ankle?" He wasn't sure why he asked because he had no idea if it would do anything, with the exception of perhaps increase circulation.

But he knew she needed something to make her less sad, to distract her.

"We can try."

He shifted to face her legs and feet. *Here goes.*

Wrapping his hands around her right foot, he applied light pressure, being extra careful around the ankle.

"This okay?"

"Yes. Nice, actually."

He continued, thinking he was at least doing something positive. And truth be told, he liked having his hands on her. Not that he'd admit that out loud. She'd be liable to haul off and punch him. Little dynamo.

"Can you do my calf, too?"

He smiled, and worked his hands up her calf to her knee.

Her head dropped back against the sofa.

Well, that was surprising. He would've bet his last Jackson that she'd throw the ice at him, and tell him to take a hike.

He watched her angelic face as he worked on her muscles. Her features softened, and her lips parted as the tension evaporated from her body.

Shit! He loved the look of her face in simple relaxation.

His heart beat stronger with every glide up and down her leg. On a whim, he moved one hand to her left calf, now working both simultaneously.

She let out a soft groan. "God, that feels good." Then she reached for the remote and silenced the TV.

Fuck! As much as he'd wished she shut him down, he equally wanted to keep his hands on her. Anywhere on her.

He swallowed hard. His hands may have crept a little higher, past her knees several inches. The devil in him offered no apologies.

"Mmm."

Double fuck! He should stop. In another five or six seconds, she would likely chew his ass out. He counted in his head, but the time came and went.

Her skin was like silk under his rough fingertips. He licked his lips. He didn't know if he could trust himself to continue without potentially crossing the line.

"Feeling better?" he asked, trying to keep his voice calm.

"Yes." She opened her eyelids half-way.

If he didn't know better, he'd think she'd reached a point beyond relaxation.

"Please, don't stop," she said, pleading with those beautiful hazel eyes.

He bit down on the inside of his cheek. "Liddy."

"Please," she begged, but he couldn't be sure for what.

Meanwhile, the erection in his pants grew to a painful level. Second time in as many days.

Fuck. This woman had an effect on him.

He stroked her soft legs, willing his damn hands to stop. His fingertips skimmed her boxer shorts.

She didn't move a muscle. In fact, she may have sunk lower in her seat. All he could hear was her gentle pants.

The blanket fell to the floor, and still she didn't object. *Think.*

"Liddy, are you sure you don't want me to stop? Because if you don't, I'm not sure how far I'll go," he confessed in a low tone.

She opened her darkened hazel eyes, meeting his gaze head-on. "Don't stop, Luke."

Fuck me! His dick nearly jerked for joy at those world-stopping words. As he searched for an excuse to leave, his hands had their own ideas. He inched higher, wrapping his hands around those toned thighs. He stroked rhythmically up and down, slowly climbing higher and carefully pushing against her left leg, giving him access.

When she didn't stop him, he knew there was no turning

back. Her breath came quicker from those beautiful, parted lips.

Going on feel alone, he glossed over her tender flesh through the boxers.

Her chest rose in an inhale.

He dared to go farther, and slid the tip of a finger gently into the side of the fabric, and up her wet slit.

Her sex was wet and warm. Smooth as silk. What he wouldn't give to see for himself.

With two fingers, he trailed a path along her slit, gathering her moisture to spread higher. When he glazed over her hard, delectable numb, her back bowed slightly, arching into his hand.

He made small circles with his right hand over her eager clit, and played over her lips with the left. The more he played, the slicker she grew.

She moaned on an exhale.

Maneuvering against her boxers, he slowly drove one, then two fingers inside her tight channel. She felt like pure heaven. He continued his ministrations on her clit while she arched against his hand and gripped the sofa.

He pushed in, curling his fingers on the way out, all while circling her hot little button.

"Luke," she panted.

"Let go, sweet cheeks."

Another second passed, and her face flushed, so delectable. Her chest rose and fell with every exquisite breath.

She cried out as she splintered before him—a beautiful sight by any measure.

After several long seconds, she sagged in her seat, sated and satisfied. Even her mouth looked full, her face flushed, and oh so kissable.

He carefully fixed her boxers and stood to re-cover her with the blanket.

She opened her eyes to look at him—beautifully flushed face and lids at half-mast.

He couldn't help himself. He leaned over and crushed his lips to hers. He kissed her the way this woman was supposed to be kissed. He fucking loved what she'd just given him, and loved that she trusted him enough to let him do it.

Regrettably, he broke away from the lust-filled kiss. He'd love nothing more than to worship Liddy from head to toe, but she wasn't ready for that, if at all. He had to get his ass out of there.

"Ice for twenty minutes, sweet cheeks." Then he straightened, went to the door, and gently closed it behind him. Time to release this absolute agony in his pants, with either a cold shower, or a fantasy dream in his room. An awesome moment he'd replay a thousand times.

WAS SHE OUT of her mind? Liddy sat on the sofa, just as Luke had left her, the tingles of her orgasm still reverberating throughout her.

That was the craziest thing I've ever done.

What came over her? She hated the man. His ridiculous, childish jokes, the dry sarcasm, the way he walked around like he owned everything, as if the world revolved around him.

But she almost hated herself more—for finding his touch that erotic. That delicious. So invigorating.

Dammit, she cursed herself for wanting more of it.

This trip wasn't about finding romance or a distraction—this vacation was for her mental health, for rest and relaxation. Hadn't she told herself to give men a rest? The past decade worth of mistakes had shown her a break from men was long overdue. Always clinging to a lover like that was the sole of her existence, suffocating the relationship until it died, and then immediately searching for the next one.

Social workers had forced her into a few therapy sessions as a young child during her foster years. They claimed her neediness was a common side effect, constantly searching for love and acceptance with a strong aversion to rejection, which had described a lot of her behaviors over the years.

Liddy refused to be a statistic. She'd created a damn good life for herself, and it was no easy feat.

The minute she'd stopped focusing on love all together, fate dropped a painful injury in her lap, topped off with the sexiest, most infuriating man she'd ever laid eyes on for a nurse.

Mmm, some bedside manner!

Chapter SEVEN

THE AMAZING INTERLUDE with Liddy refused to stay in the back of Luke's mind. He still had a lot of work to do, but her gorgeously flushed face as she reached her peak kept popping back up in his imagination. He could still feel her hot sex pulsing around his fingers. There was just no way he could concentrate.

"I'm not paying for this!" an angry guest barked from the other side of the counter.

Luke glanced up. He'd only come out to the front to use the printer, but it was at the wrong moment. The man complained—loudly—about line item charges on their bill.

Charice, the client relations manager, maintained her composure well and tried to diffuse the man's combative attitude as she'd taken over for Russell, who helped another couple check in, his smile still in place. Charice's smile was bright against her dark skin. Her trimmed fingernails flew over the keyboard from years of experience in the hospitality industry.

Luke grabbed the stack of release forms off the printer, keeping his glances discreet but ready to step in to back her up, just in case.

The guest and his wife were in their late fifties, their expensive attire pristinely pressed, and the woman's hair teased to perfection. From the designer watch on the man's wrist, and the two-carat diamonds dangling from his wife's ears—with the gaudiest ring dazzling off her finger—the couple could've afforded anything they wanted in life. Just like Luke. Yet, they picked over some miniscule charges and resort taxes.

That mentality was widespread among his family's circles back in New York—an attitude Luke was grateful he'd escaped from years before.

Life was just far too short to fuss over the piddly shit.

Instead, Luke focused on collecting experiences, relationships, and those rare connections that made a person truly priceless.

Charice managed to help the guests, and they eventually left satisfied.

Luke patted her on the shoulder as he walked by. "Well done."

"Not my first rodeo," she sighed. "But I'll definitely put them on the blacklist. They were just out for a bunch of freebies."

"Sorry. Keep your chin up. I hear the chefs are pulling out all the stops for the Thanksgiving dinner tomorrow."

Charice sighed. "I can almost smell their cranberry sauce."

Luke dashed off to the coffee shop for his usual afternoon pick-me-up, today's special being cinnamon dolce coffee. He picked up a few extras, and dropped one off for Charice.

She gasped. "You are so sweet! How are you that good at reading my mind?"

"I stalk you on social media. You just wrote *#NeedACoffee*, and *#FirstWorldProblems*."

She laughed. "Thank you, Luke. If I weren't already married . . ."

"You'd turn right back around and ask him to marry you again. Don't lie." Luke tapped the stack of papers on her keyboard. "Cuz if you don't, then I would. Your husband makes the best smoked brisket. I'd switch sides for that alone. Don't go giving that up."

Charice laughed.

"Wait, you're switching sides?" Russell piped up, his smile super bright.

"Not today, my friend. But be patient. One day, your prince will come." Luke set one of the extra coffees in front of him. "In the meantime, this'll keep you warm."

Russell sighed, and breathed in the cinnamon scent. "I can dream. Thanks for the hit of caffeine."

A shout echoed from the down the hall, followed by a few curse words.

Charice stepped into the hall to see what was wrong.

Luke grinned, and leaned against the wall.

Patrick, fellow ski instructor and his closest friend for the last three years, stood outside the instructor's office they all shared. Covered in packing peanuts. "Dammit, Sawyer!" he bellowed. He kicked out a bunch more from the office. "I'm not cleaning this up!"

"What did you do?" Luke feigned concern.

Charice walked down the hall, peered into the office, and burst out laughing.

Luke had filled the office with packing peanuts and bubble paper on Patrick's time slot for desk hours as his latest prank.

"Is this from all the new skies and equipment we got in?" His friend asked, brushing off the foam stuck to his clothes.

"Yeah. That's what you get for skipping dish duty last week."

Patrick's face flushed red. "You're such a jackass! Come clean this up."

Luke glanced at his wrist, sans watch. "I've got a class of newbies to teach. Work comes first. Have fun!" With a wink, he turned and walked off.

"Sawyer!" his friend barked after him.

"You are such a troublemaker." Charice crossed her arms over her pristine suit with the resort logo on the lapel. She grinned ear to ear.

"He likes it," Luke whispered back. "That's hours of free

fun, popping all that bubble wrap."

His phone buzzed in his pocket. Caller ID showed his sister, Chloe.

"What do you know, my favorite sister." He smirked as he answered, imagining her smirking on the other end, too.

"Well, you're not my favorite brother right now." Similar voice to their mother, with a sharper tongue.

"What did I do now?" He rounded the corner and grabbed his coat from the employee breakroom. If he was going to get an earful from Chloe, might as well do it away from guests.

"I just got off the phone with Mom. She says you're not coming home this week?"

He opened the door to the outside, the cold breeze stinging his face as he walked. "It's been a whole day since that call with her, Chloe. You're losing your touch. I expected my phone to ring even before I hung up with Mom." A few people waved at him, newbies from his lessons yesterday. He waved back with a smile, but turned the corner around the building back toward the patio which was vacant this time of year.

His sister scoffed on the other end. "Some of us work for a living, Luke. Not spend our days on holiday."

"Well, that's a lesson you haven't learned yet. Do something you love, and you'll never work a day in your life."

"Listen. There's a really important thing Mom and Dad wanted to talk to you about in person. They were counting on you to be here."

"And, Mom can't talk to me over the phone about it?"

"She wants to hand over the reins on the foundation. The workload has become too much for her, and they want someone with business savvy to take over, someone they trust."

"Since when has the foundation ever been too much work?"

"When the scope increased ten-fold, and the budget quadrupled. It's not just a little charity anymore, Luke. She's happy being the spokeswoman, but you know her. She won't admit to needing help until she's a thousand leagues under the sea. You already know the business side of things. You're the best choice."

The clouds shifted with the breeze, revealing a rare glimpse of sunshine. The blanket of snow on the mountain became an instant dazzling array of color, light bouncing off the fractals against the tree line. He pulled his sunglasses down to shield his eyes, but he loved watching how everyone on the mountain simultaneously stopped to enjoy the same view.

"Luke? Are you listening?"

"Yes, I hear you," he sighed. "How can you say I'm that best choice? I've been gone ten years."

"That part's irrelevant. Mom's already made all the connections."

"Was this Mom's idea, or Dad's? Or yours?"

"Does it matter? You need to come home."

"I can't come home this week. I already have commitments here. But I promise to think about the offer."

"What commitments? Skiing lessons? Don't you think family is more important?"

He pulled off his sunglasses, as if she could look into his eyes to see how much that comment irritated him. "Chloe, I love you. Have a good Thanksgiving. I'll call you later."

He hung up without waiting for her response.

Nothing ruined a beautiful day faster than a call from his older, overbearing sister. She was very much the spitting image of their mother, but with the hard-edge acumen of their father, everything down to brass-tacks.

Damn, life was far too serious at that level of intensity. At least far too serious for Luke.

He slipped his sunglasses back on and looked up just in time to see Liddy's friends walking from the lift, done with the slopes for the day. Rosy cheeks, fun smiles, and exhausted feet.

Seeing her friends reminded Luke of the sinful desire in cabin eight, and the stellar moment they had with her on the sofa, his fingers making her come so hard.

Yeah, the commitments here are far more important.

Chapter EIGHT

THE NEXT DAY, Liddy's friends clomped through the front door of the cabin, both sporting pink noses.

"How was skiing?" Liddy twisted on the sofa to face the door.

"Awesome," Sam replied with a smile.

"That light snowfall last night made the runs great today." Jordan stripped out of her hat, gloves, jacket, and sat to pull off her ski boots. "Even tried out a new black diamond today. Wide open."

Sam nodded. "Great powder."

Liddy licked her lips, trying to hold back a pang of envy. The slopes had called her even before she left San Francisco. But the *encounter* with Luke the prior day provided a surprisingly sufficient distraction.

Jordan stood. "So tonight, how about we make a pitcher of margaritas, sour cream chicken enchiladas, and watch Friday the 13th, just for you." She gave Liddy her brightest smile.

Liddy couldn't help but laugh. "Great idea. Love it."

She lifted herself on her crutches and hobbled to the kitchen.

"We can do it," Sam said as she frowned.

"No, I'll help some. At least give me something to cut." Liddy plopped herself onto a barstool. "Plus, doc said I can ditch the crutches soon."

"Oh, yeah." Sam grinned.

"So, how did it go for you today?" Jordan started pulling ingredients out of the fridge.

"Not too bad." She forced more positivity in her voice than she really felt.

"What did you do?" Sam asked.

"I read an entire novel, did almost the entire book of Sudoku puzzles, and watched a few movies," she supplied. Hoping the whole time Luke would check in on her.

The buzz from the body-numbing orgasm from Luke's expert fingers the prior day had faded. Liddy hated to admit it, but she missed seeing Luke. She'd dreamt about him, and the need to kiss him again was maddening.

Of course, she kept these yummy secrets to herself. What happened with Luke was a moment of weakness; it would never happen again. Given enough time on this short trip, he'd likely do something else to piss her off, like smack her ass.

Mmm. Maybe she should scratch that thought.

Damn! That man is infuriating. She couldn't even think

straight.

"Is the cabin fever getting to you?" Jordan asked with a sympathetic look. "Lord knows by now I'd be all Dragon Lady, peeling the wallpaper off the walls."

Liddy chuckled. "Good thing there's no paper on these walls. I'm good, really."

The smell of Jordan's phenomenal chicken enchiladas filled the cabin, as if they were back in San Fran munching away on Liddy's patio watching the ships sail under the Golden Gate Bridge. And she was oh-so-thankful for the distraction.

As soon as they finished, they plopped in front of the TV—Liddy in her usual spot—and turned on the horror movie, with just the light of the fire.

Not five minutes into the movie, a knock rapped on their door.

"Don't open it," Sam whispered, "It's *him*!" referring to the hockey-masked villain.

Liddy giggled as Jordan called through the door. "Who is it?"

"Room service," Luke's unmistakable voice called through the wooden panels. "Would you like me to fluff your pillows?"

Jordan grinned, her gaze locked on Liddy. "They sent your own personal nurse."

Liddy shook her head. *No, no, no!* But she was too embarrassed to speak.

Jordan opened the door.

Luke stepped onto the rug. The firelight caught glints of snow on his coat and hat. "How is our patient?"

His stare landed on her, and *damn,* that smile. Less reserved than the previous day, like he was bursting at the seams with their naughty little secret. *Bastard.*

"She's all tucked in for one of her favorites," Jordan answered, then closed the door behind him.

Liddy glared at her for using her *mama* voice, as if Liddy were a toddler.

"Jason! Superb taste. I had no idea you were into slasher films."

"My choice was Miracle on 34th Street," Sam countered, "but got overruled. Apparently, Christmas season doesn't start until Friday." She winked at Liddy.

"You're way too PG for me." Luke's stare started to get way too personal—as if he could see straight through her clothes, and Liddy's cheeks warmed at the thought.

"Oh!" Jordan's face lit up with another one of her ideas.

Liddy cringed inside for what was to come.

"It's game night at the Lodge tonight, isn't it?" She looked at Luke, then Sam.

"Not sure. Is it Wednesday?" Luke reached for his phone.

"Yep," Sam chimed in. "Charades, Pictionary, and giant Jenga."

"You know what?" Jordan pulled on her boots. "I think we're gonna head over and play for a while. Give Luke a chance to check on the patient. Liddy, sweetie, I know you're not a fan of those group games. Do you want me to bring back some dessert from the restaurant?"

"You don't have to leave," she piped up. "We just started the movie. Besides, I'm sure Luke has *a lot* more important things to do." She glared at him.

He only coughed into his hand, clearly trying to hide a chuckle.

As Sam slid her boots on, Jordan held their jackets in her hand. "We'll catch you guys later." And as fast as that, the door slammed shut.

Those two will pay.

"Let's check out the ankle. See if you can ditch the crutches." Luke knelt down at her feet like the day before.

"So, did you go to medical school or something?"

"No. I majored in business, with a minor in kinesiology. But I've seen enough of these injuries over the years."

She nodded.

He pressed in a few spots on her foot and ankle. "Does this hurt?"

"No."

He asked several more times. Each time, she gave the same answer.

"It looks pretty good, Liddy. I'd say you can hit the slopes tomorrow. Take it easy, though, and warm up first."

She found herself staring at his mouth as he spoke. He had some of the nicest lips she'd ever seen on a man.

He lifted his eyebrows like he was waiting on her response.

Oh! "Good news. I'll get skis in the morning. Maybe I can at least get one good day of skiing in before we leave."

"You head home on Friday now?"

She nodded.

"Good." He stepped back and sat in the club chair facing her. "So, what's your story, Liddy? Do you have a boyfriend waiting for you back in San Francisco?"

She turned to look at the fire.

"My friends say I'm clingy, and I chase them away." Liddy instantly bit her tongue, stunned that she would admit that out loud. To *him,* of all people. This had to be the pain killers talking.

"Do you think you're clingy?" he asked.

"No, but does any woman think that?"

His lips pulled to the side as if considering her statement. "Let's see. Do you call them more than once a day?"

She sighed. "Well, yes."

"Do you text him an unnecessarily large amount of times?"

"What's unnecessarily large?"

"That's a yes." He crossed his arms. "Do you overanalyze what he posts on social media?"

She glanced off to the side, thinking about the last time she'd done that. Perhaps overanalyzed wasn't the right description, but she definitely stewed over possible meanings, yeah.

"I could go on, but it definitely looks like you're in the clinger zone."

Her chin lifted. "I think you're really over-simplifying it. And this isn't *all* my fault."

He leaned forward resting his elbows on his legs. "Those guys got it wrong."

She blinked. *He's going to take my side?*

"They don't know how to handle that kind of attention. If you were mine, I'd leave you each morning telling you exactly what I'd do to you when I get home. You would be so wet and wanting, you wouldn't have time to guess if you were on my mind all day or not. Thinking about you or someone else. You would always know where you stood with me."

Oh, shit.

Well, yes, if she had a man like that, she would definitely *not* wonder. A man who told her, under no uncertain terms, where she stood. A man who made her the center of his world, and relished being the center of hers.

He rose from the chair and knelt beside her, forcing her gaze higher. His fingertips pushed her hair away from her eyes and trailed down her cheek. His thumb brushed across her lips, and she couldn't think straight.

He stared, watching her face, like he debated his next move.

Kiss me.

He didn't. Instead, he lifted her feet off the ottoman,

setting them on the floor. Then he pushed the ottoman off to the side and knelt between her legs.

"Liddy, there is something about you I can't put my finger on. You have the most angelic face with beautiful, pouty pink lips, and yet you like slasher movies. You wear fuzzy sweaters with purple leggings," he glanced down at her attire, "and cuss like a sailor."

His hand caressed her skin once again. "When I look at you, all I can think about is how badly I want to kiss you."

Yes.

She wished like hell she didn't want it so much, but she did. She wanted him to kiss her, caress her, show her the passion that didn't just simmer under the surface, but boiled and bubbled.

And she wanted to do the very same things back to him.

"I won't stop you," she whispered, then hooked her good foot around his leg.

Without hesitation, he plunged his firm lips over hers, taking whatever he wanted, taking all she could give.

Her arms swung around his shoulders, her fingers threading through his hair.

His tongue tangled with hers. Then he tipped her head, taking the kiss deeper.

The dampness in her panties grew.

This wholly masculine man overwhelmed her, tantalized her, made lust unfurl inside her. She wanted more. Needed more. So much more than a mere distraction.

His evergreen scent held a hint of cardamom, and the minty taste of his lips clouded her brain—her friends wouldn't be gone nearly long enough.

"Luke," she panted, turning her head as he laid kisses down her neck.

"Don't tell me to stop. Please." He pulled back to meet her gaze, lust brimming from his eyes.

"I wasn't going to."

"Thank God," he touched his forehead to hers.

"How long does game night last? How long do we have?"

He grinned. "Hours. I have a condom."

Thank God. She pulled herself into him, claiming his lips.

His hands slid down her sides and yanked her sweater over her, causing her hair to fall in every direction. "Sweetheart, I'm going to make you feel so good."

She mewled when he pulled her in close to the erection pressing against his jeans. She couldn't recall ever wanting a man so much.

She yanked at his shirt, whipping it over his head.

With his lips on her neck, he whispered in between kisses, "Lift."

She boosted her hips off the sofa as he grabbed her leggings, pushing them to the floor.

"God, you're beautiful." He wrapped his arms around her waist, and holding her close, he lowered her to the floor.

She ran her hands down his smooth chest while he

reached behind her and snapped loose her bra.

"Fuck," he said under his breath as her hands wandered over his erection, caressing him through his jeans.

He grabbed her hands and held them against the rug on the floor over her head, and in an instant his mouth was on her nipple.

"Unh," she cried out when he sucked her hard nipple, the electricity shooting south.

He treated her other nipple the same way, and with her hands pinned, there was nothing she could do but take the exquisite torture. She wrapped her legs around him, feeling the slickness at her sex. She gripped her legs tight around him, pressing her center against his, dying to relieve the throb.

"Sweet cheeks, I think you just might like it a bit kinky. Am I right?"

What? "Um, I don't know."

He grinned as he waggled his eyebrows. "Only one way to find out."

He reached for her tank top. "Do you trust me?"

She didn't know why, but . . . "Yes."

"Close your eyes." As she did, he placed the cotton top over her eyes and tied it on the side, creating a blindfold. "Comfortable?"

She nodded.

His hands stroked up and down her thighs to her torso, and on the last pass downward, he grabbed ahold of her pink satin thong, and yanked it off her legs.

"Sweet Jesus," he breathed.

Not being able to see what he was doing only heightened her other senses. In the dark, she focused on his touch, the rough pads on his fingertips sent tingles along her skin in his wake. Her heart rate sped, and she panted gently.

With his hands on her thighs, pushing almost to the point of pain, he made himself room to devour her.

His warm tongue finally claimed her, pressing against her clit, playing her like an instrument of sex, thriving on vibration.

"Luke," she called out. The heat escalated so fast, the coil in her body tightened almost instantly.

He sent her to the stars in mere seconds. "Ah," she cried when her climax slammed through her unexpectedly.

She lay panting, getting her bearings, mildly aware of the rustling of Luke stripping out of his clothes and the crinkle of a condom wrapper.

"I want to see you," she pleaded.

"Soon." He pecked her lips and whispered, "On your knees, sweet cheeks."

She gathered herself and flipped over to rest on all fours, presenting her backside to him.

His hand smoothed on her bare ass. He leaned forward, caressing his cock along her sex. Over and over his warm hand made circles over her ass.

"This has to be the finest ass I've ever seen."

Slap!

She squealed.

"Or slapped."

Her heart thundered, and she bit her lip on the ecstasy.

Then without another word, he dove into her.

They both groaned aloud, unabashedly.

His hand slid up her back along her spine, stroking her, seducing her. "Fuck, angel, you feel amazing."

He pushed her hair to the side, uncovering her neck. He licked, kissed, and left a trail of little bites along her back, sending shivers across her skin.

And his thrusts. God, he moved like he knew exactly what she needed, slowly taking another inch until he reached her end. Then back out again, increasing the tempo with each slide—as if he could feel her pulse inside, and dragged out the pleasure for every achingly delicious second. It took only a few short moments before she felt the beginnings of another orgasm build deep inside.

"Luke. Luke," she chanted.

"Yes, baby." He slid his fingers up her back to the base of her neck. The other hand gently gripping, increasing the pressure at her ass, and building her higher.

When the climax hit, she cried out. Her body came undone in every direction, her inhibitions completely unraveled and basking in the vibrations echoing throughout her limbs. She rested her head against the floor and pushed back against him.

He pulled out, yanked off the blindfold, and rolled her

onto her back.

Oh God, he was beautiful. So perfect. The man's body was tone with defined abs and muscular legs. What had her heart skipping like a downhill skier on a black diamond was his cock—the thick girth, eager for more of her.

"I need to kiss you," he breathed over her lips, claiming her again.

Even though her arms and legs shook, she wrapped around him as he entered her, filling the emptiness from just seconds before. The tightness in her ankle shot low-grade pain up her calf, but she didn't care. He felt too damn good.

His tongue danced with hers in a hungry, passionate kiss. She craved his kiss, the feel of him inside her, his hard body moving with hers.

Another orgasm rose close to the surface, but wouldn't tip over—dangling her at the edge of bliss, teasing her. Taunting her. She didn't care. She'd already had two.

Before she could think any more about it, Luke rolled to the floor, bringing her on top of him. Her legs straddled him, riding him like a saddle. "One more, angel, before I explode."

His thumb slid over her engorged clit.

"Oh," she gasped. Oh, his movements, the pressure, everything he did to her felt so consuming. Her fingers scraped along his chest, grabbing for something to hold herself steady.

His hips rocked into her, sending him deeper into her core. Combined with the relentless circling on her nub, the quickening built fast.

She leaned back, supporting herself with her hands on his shins. Her quads stretched, pulling against her ankle, pushing the pressure higher. She pulsed over him, grinding against his thumb.

"Oh, God." She was delirious with pleasure. "Luke."

The inner coil sprung loose, and tipped her over that sweet edge. Another climax broke free. She arched her back, crying out.

Something else released, but Liddy couldn't recognize it in her ecstasy.

Luke called out her name as he gripped her hips, grinding out his release at the same time.

She collapsed to his chest, clinging to his body for balance.

They laid there, panting, for several moments.

When she regained the energy, she pinched his arm.

"Ow," he muttered. "What was that for?"

"Make sure you're real." *And to verify the best sex of my life wasn't a dream.*

He chuckled. "It has to be the other way around for that." He slid his hand between them, and gently pinched her nipple.

The pain was pleasurable. "Mmm. Yep, this is real."

Chapter NINE

DEEP IN HIS gut, Luke knew he'd just had the best fucking sex of his life. Liddy was amazing, sensual, and on fire under his touch.

After several minutes, she lifted off his chest, and although he wanted her there forever, they were still connected.

"That was amazing. Is three orgasms in an hour your record on a woman?"

He grinned. "The record I want to take credit for is far more impressive."

"What?"

His smile grew. "Baby, you squirted."

She blinked. "I *what*?" She looked down at the sheen of fluid left on his groin. The lustful look instantly vanished, replaced by unmistakable embarrassment. "Ohmigod, I thought that was just a myth."

"That, I will absolutely take credit for." His face started to hurt from smiling so much. He cupped her cheeks. "Just proves how fucking incredible you are."

"Holy crap!" She giggled, grazing her fingertips over the crux of his upper thigh.

He'd be in trouble if she kept that up. "Sweet cheeks, will you get us some towels?"

She did as he asked, returning to help clean them both. Then she laid next to him, resting her head on his chest.

Luke couldn't explain the comfort this simple position gave him. The fling with Liddy was temporary—long distance fuck buddies at best—and he couldn't define why she, of all the women he'd known, had such an incredible effect on him.

He absently kissed the top of her head. "Are you one of those closet nymphos? Refuse to let on that you like it hard and kinky?"

She was too exhausted to laugh. "I had no idea. Wasn't brought up that way."

He chuckled. "Restrictive parents?"

Liddy tensed in his arms. "Actually, my parents were pretty supportive."

"You're telling me you're the only person on the planet who had a normal childhood?"

She snorted. "There was *nothing* normal about it." Then she rose onto her elbow.

He watched her carefully, ready to hear the punchline, when he registered the sincerity in her face.

Her hair tumbled over her shoulder, and skimmed his chin. He tucked it back behind her ear.

"I guess you had pretty restrictive parents," she continued, "given your *observation* on me. But that's probably because they really cared, and wanted the best for you."

His mouth turned a little dry. She had no idea who his family was, or their motivations. But he wasn't sure where she was going with her line of thinking either. "Is this a lecture?"

She shook her head. "No. Just . . . not many people get that kind of support as a kid. I sure didn't. Not until after I was ten years old and had gone through six foster homes. By that point, I'd already seen a lot of shit."

Liddy pushed herself off him, and reached for the quilt, pulling it around her body.

He yanked on his briefs and sat up as well—putting effort into making sure his body language and close proximity conveyed he wasn't going to run away.

They stared at the crackling fire, sitting in silence for several moments.

Liddy's body tensed, her shoulders drawing up against her neck.

Luke recognized the defensive body language. He wouldn't let her close herself off. He wrapped his arm around her. "You don't have to get so guarded. I won't judge you, ever. Tell me about it."

"I don't think you want to hear a pity party."

"I want to hear *everything* about you. No pity involved."

How could I pity this fascinating woman?

She tried to hold back a derisive look, but failed. That glorious face held a lot of anguish behind it. "I have no idea who my real father is, and based on my biological mother's choices for drugs and prostitution, I doubt even she knows who he is. When I was six, she left me outside a liquor store, and never came back. CPS finally picked me up after a week of wandering the streets, and I bounced around foster homes for a few years. Until Holly House intervened and assigned me to the right couple, who eventually adopted me."

Luke sat and listened, careful not to reveal any change in his emotions. He couldn't describe just how much he admired someone like her for overcoming those experiences.

"I'd spent about a year with them when they sat me down in their dining room one day, with my case manager," she explained further. "I fully expected them to tell me they couldn't care for me anymore, and were kicking me out to another foster family. That's when they slid the official adoption papers across the table. Asked me to be a part of their family permanently. Best day of my life."

"When you were ten?"

She nodded. And stayed silent.

A dozen emotions flickered across her exquisite face, the most obvious one was defensive. As if she expected him to bolt, to reject her for having a less than perfect childhood.

Luke almost hated himself after hearing that story. He'd had it so much easier than most, especially compared to foster kids. But he could certainly understand that fear of rejection, after the fiasco with Ashley.

How anyone could reject this dazzling woman in front of him, so hungry and open to life, was beyond him.

"I can't imagine how difficult that life must've been," he finally gathered his words enough to respond. "I have no idea what happened to you as a kid in those foster homes, but I promise I'm the last person to ever judge someone based on their past."

"How can you honestly say that? Someone's past is full of all their choices, all their decisions. It's who they are."

Luke smiled, trying hard to keep the rancor from bubbling up. "Your past is *not* who you are. Your family, or lack thereof, and the things that happened *to* you do not define you." He'd tried so hard for ten years to make sure of that. He was *not* his family. "The way you treat people, and the things you say, and the choices you make *right now* make up who you are." He pulled her legs over his lap, refusing to allow her to shut herself down. "Like your decision to let a funny, handsome, creative—"

"Arrogant..."

He shrugged. "Sometimes, and starved sex-fiend into your cabin."

She smirked. "Some might call that reckless."

"I call it knowing what you want." *Damn,* how he desperately wanted another round with Liddy.

"If you know what you want, how come some hot ski bunny hasn't landed you yet?"

"Because I've been burned before. So, I like to keep things casual. I'm a simple guy with simple demands. I don't place a lot of needs on others for that reason."

"Don't want to get burned again, huh? Sounds familiar. Who was she? College sweetheart or another guest at the resort?"

An image of Ashley's platinum hair and that dreadful night after graduation flashed in his mind. "Someone who made me grow up a bit. Made me a little wiser, too."

"Who also made it harder for you to trust people, right?" It was a question that didn't require an answer.

He tilted his head. "Does that sound familiar?"

"A bit," she replied with a modest shrug.

Luke chewed on the inside of his lip. *Should I tell her? Can I trust her?* The idea floated around in his mind for half a second, wondering if he could let down his guard enough to give her the full picture of who he really was.

"Are you hungry?" she asked.

"Starving." He let the idea fade, probably not the right time anyway. That could wait. "Let's dig around in the pantry for some fuel, and then get dressed. I have something I want to show you."

Her eyebrows nearly hit her hairline. "Now?"

He nodded, glancing at the darkness out the windows. "Right now."

Liddy gingerly walked to the kitchen and pulled out food from the fridge.

He loved watching her work. "You're moving well."

"It feels good to walk again. We have some chicken enchiladas left. How's that?"

"Sounds delicious. What can I do to help?"

"I got it. Make yourself at home."

He mostly ate, while she munched on chips and salsa, watching him.

"So, why on the floor, Sawyer?"

He stopped mid-bite and looked over at her. "What?"

"Why did you move me to the floor?"

"I like space. To move around. The sofa is too confining," he said with an unapologetic grin plastered to his face. "I enjoy your kinky side."

"Me too," she whispered. She slid off the barstool. "Want some more water?"

She didn't wait for a reply, and refilled both glasses. "If we're going somewhere, I'm getting dressed."

"Good idea." Although secretly, he loved knowing she was naked under that blanket, and would happily keep her that way for the rest of the night.

He stacked his dishes in the dishwasher and dressed himself. She exited the bedroom in jeans and a sweater. Then he handed her the white ski jacket from the hook by the door. "C'mon."

She gave him an uncertain look. "You know I probably shouldn't walk too far."

"I know, sweet cheeks. It's close by. Or I can always carry

you."

She rolled her eyes.

Chapter TEN

ONLY A FEW steps outside the cabin and all the after-sex heat engulfing Liddy's body had dissipated. The cold mountain air turned frigid in the middle of the night, with the breeze kicking up, sucking out the high from their hot monkey-sex on the rug.

She pulled the hood over her face tighter, hoping to savor any remaining warmth.

"Just take it slow." Luke held her hand as she traversed up the snow-covered path until they reached the tree line. The wind calmed behind the shield of towering pines.

Barely out of breath, Liddy spotted their destination—a clearing toward the top of a hill. The area was probably a popular destination during the day for hikers and bird watchers with several benches alongside a few doused campfires encircled by stones.

But at night, it was too dark to see more than a dozen paces.

Why did he bring me here?

He sat her down on a bench, the glimmer on his face like a secret only he knew about. "Look up."

Stars sparkled across the sky like God let off a glitter bomb in the heavens.

Liddy's mouth fell open.

Away from the light pollution of San Francisco, and in the mountains, they seemed closer to the sky—almost close enough to reach out and touch each star.

"This is one of my favorite things out here," Luke explained. "I could never see this many stars back in New York."

New York? Somewhere urban, most likely, she thought as she continued to marvel at the constellations.

She pointed at a cluster of stars. "There's Ursa Minor. And the Draco constellation, oh my gosh! I never see these back home."

"You know constellations?"

She grinned. "One of my foster fathers was big into astronomy, but the lighting was never right to observe most of these. Look there! Gemini! It's so bright up here."

"Reminds me of a Jackson Pollock painting." Luke sat beside her, their bodies touching from shoulder to knee. "Like he just flung a bunch of white and yellow paint splotches against a black canvas."

Liddy nodded. "Explosions in the sky."

"You could call it that."

"No," she chuckled. "The song, "Explosions in the Sky.""

That's what this needs. A soundtrack."

"I'm not familiar with that one. But here's one for the playlist, Flock of Seagulls, "Space Age Love Song.""

He looked so proud of himself with that statement, she could only laugh. "You're an eighties movies fan, aren't you?"

Luke shrugged. "Some of them."

"I've got you beat."

He turned and straddled the bench, pulling her into him. "You can try." Little puffs came out of his mouth as he spoke, the warmth on her face so enticing.

"Black Sabbath's, "Laguna Sunrise.""

His grin widened. "That's impressive. How about Guns N' Roses, "Sweet Child O' Mine.""

"That'll work. But we can't leave out Bruce Springsteen. "Dancing in the Dark," nothing more relevant for stargazing than that."

""Beth," by KISS," he whispered, leaning in closer to steal one from her lips.

Liddy wrapped her arm around his shoulder. ""Beast of Burden." Rolling Stones."

Luke gasped. "You're a woman after my own heart." He glanced up one more time, then met her gaze. "I think you are the first woman I've met who knows astronomy. And has the *best* taste in music."

Even in the dark, his eyes held that unmistakable twinkle. She'd once thought it fake, but she'd come to learn it was absolutely authentic.

She shivered.

"You're getting cold. We should head back."

She nodded. As much as she savored the expanse of beauty above them, freezing to death wasn't a smart move.

He held her close the whole way down the path, until the last several paces when the ache intensified in her calf. She stumbled a bit.

Luke didn't hesitate. He scooped her up, and carried her the rest of the way, up the three steps and inside the cabin.

His heady scent magnified. This close, she noticed his hair was slightly longer on top than the back and a hint of stubble outlined his chin.

He gently set her down in the entryway, with a constant hold on her arm.

She relished the heat, as if it were a safety net to loneliness.

He stared down into her eyes.

She could barely breathe.

"Liddy—"

"My full name is Lydia," she interrupted, not entirely sure why she needed to share.

Stupid Liddy. Going back to babbling nonsense when enamored with a guy.

"Lydia." He smiled. "I like that. Do you prefer Lydia?"

She forced a tiny breath. The way her name came off his lips did so many things to her heart. "I'm good either way."

He helped her out of her coat, and hung it on the wall.

"I'd like to try and ski with you awhile tomorrow, Lydia. Make sure your ankle is strong enough."

"Okay." The thought gave her some much-needed comfort and peace of mind. She was nervous about being on the slopes again, and concerned that she could do permanent damage.

"The Lodge is cooking up Thanksgiving dinner for guests. Afterward, will you spend time with me? Alone?"

Her stomach flip-flopped, and then fluttered like fairies on caffeine. "Okay."

He gave her his brilliant smile, cupped the sides of her head, and kissed her. His lips were firm, warm and inviting.

She stepped closer into him, savoring the feel of his body pressed against hers.

"Tomorrow," he exhaled.

"See you then," she whispered, too breathless to smile.

He opened the door, and there stood Jordan, arm stretched out for the handle.

Her eyes twinkled brighter than the Big Dipper. "Hi, Luke."

"Hi, Jordan. Sam." He nodded and cleared his throat. He cast a sly smile back at Liddy, then sidled past them.

"Bye, Luke," Sam giggled, and closed the door. Her friends stood there, staring at her with all-too-knowing grins.

"What gives?" Liddy asked. Heat flushed her face to near-burning levels.

"Uh-uh. That's our question," Jordan started.

Sam's eyes practically danced, some overly-suggestive shimmy that screamed Marvin Gaye. "Liddy found herself a ski bum."

"Yup. A hot ski bum with probably hot features *everywhere* to match."

Liddy bit the inside of her cheek under her friends' scrutiny. They had no idea how right they were.

She shook her head. "A lady never tells."

Jordan stepped around her and looked at the living room floor. The ottoman was askew, the blankets strewn all over the place, and—Liddy nearly crawled under the coffee table—a small wet spot on the area rug by the sofa.

J's eyebrows nearly hit the ceiling. "You don't have to tell. The evidence shows you're guilty, missy."

"Sure does." Sam gave her a wink, and they shrugged out of their coats. "Well done," she strung out a low seductive tone.

It took all of Liddy's strength not to cringe. There was no point in hiding it, the proof was overwhelming.

Sam headed to the bedroom for the night. Jordan gave her one of those proud mama smiles, and followed Sam down the hallway.

Thank God. At least they'd give her a reprieve until daylight, where they no doubt would grill her on Luke's prowess.

Liddy smoothed her lips together, replaying the entire night. The entire delicious, unexpected night. She hadn't meant to tell her story, but he'd listened the whole time, taking it all in. She fully expected he'd run. She could visualize the entire thing—he'd put on his clothes, make some excuse about an early morning class, grab his coat, and slam the door behind him.

She'd waited. Giving him the opportunity to run.

But he didn't. His expression was so damn handsome, but impossible to read.

Not his normal cocky smile, or arrogant smirk, but not worried or standoffish either.

What the hell had he been thinking?

There was a reason she rarely told her story. Sam and Jordan knew, sure. Her parents and everyone at Holly House knew, but boyfriends, or in this case lovers, *never* knew her past.

She couldn't put her finger on why she'd told him about her childhood. Maybe knowing their relationship would go nowhere, and she wouldn't see him again after Friday.

Her heart hurt a little with that last thought. She rubbed the wrinkle from her brow as she pushed the ottoman back in place.

She really needed to learn to not get so attached so damn quickly.

"Fuck," she said under her breath as she folded the blanket.

Yet, this dalliance with Luke somehow felt different. She'd swooned over Frank, lost sleep over Billy, and lest she not forget Jacob. The man would stop responding in the middle of a text conversation and leave her hanging for hours. She could downright crawl out of her skin until she heard from him again.

Luke made her smile and spit fire all in the same breath. Around him, she somehow could let go of her fears and inhibitions. She was more grounded and at peace with herself. Again, she thought, likely a function of being a temporary romance.

But oh, what a romance. That man was insanely good with his lips, his tongue, his hands. The girls were spot on. That man was as good in bed as he was on the slopes.

And God help her for loving it so damn much.

Chapter ELEVEN

A VICIOUS BLARING woke Liddy from her dead-like slumber. She winced through opening one eye.

Jordan strolled into her room, holding out her phone with the speaker blasting Rhianna's "S&M" song. She wore her proud and snarky expression.

Liddy grabbed one of her pillows and threw it at her annoying friend.

"Wake up, lovebug. Can't let you sleep through the last day and Thanksgiving dinner."

Liddy groaned. "Sometimes I really hate you."

Jordan laughed. "But not today." She turned off the song.

Thank God.

Then plopped down next to her on the bed. "Can't you smell the bacon?"

"No," she muffled into the pillow. Quite frankly, she didn't even smell coffee.

"Oh, that's right. It's *sausage* you like!" Jordan laughed, and tickled Liddy's sides.

"Go away." Liddy buried her head under the covers.

"I'm sorry," J replied. "I'll stop. Seriously, though. You need to get up and come see the fresh snow that fell last night. You've slept long enough. We need to get you skis and hit the slopes. Then we can chow down at the Lodge for Thanksgiving dinner."

Sam came in with two cups of coffee, and set them on the bedside table. Her pale mauve sweater matched her fuzzy socks. Always so put together, even when relaxing on vacation. How Liddy envied that.

"I have a very serious question to ask you," Sam began, sitting next to her on the other side.

Liddy sat up, rubbing the sleep from her eyes—not sure if she had the mental capacity to handle one of her friend's *serious* questions.

"Someone walked into this resort only a few days ago, and said, *No men for me on this trip*. Who was that?" The words came out sincere, albeit sober, but the funny curve on her lips was unmistakable.

"Enough."

Sam grinned. "Did you have fun? I've been worried about you on this vacation."

Oh boy, was it fun.

"I knew you would like him," Jordan beamed. "What made you come around?"

"Can't I have some coffee before the inquisition?"

Sam didn't hesitate, and handed her the mug from the bedside table. She'd made it with plenty of cream and extra sugar, just the way Liddy liked it.

Liddy inhaled the first sip, or three.

"Why'd you change your mind?" Sam asked.

"I have no idea," she admitted. "We were sitting on the couch, and he asked me if I had a boyfriend. Somehow that turned into discussing how I'm clingy, and drive men away. And instead of him running for the hills . . . he kissed me. One thing led to another . . ."

Jordan grinned.

Sam blinked. "And you're surprised?"

Liddy gawked at her friend. "How could I *not* be? With how rude I'd been to him, and downright . . ."

"Bitchy?" Jordan finished for her. "You were playing hard to get without even knowing it."

"You are, by far, the most adorable of the three of us. Probably in this whole resort." Sam motioned with an outstretched arm. "He'd be *blind* not to want you."

"But this feels different. I can't put my finger on why."

"Oh, that's easy. Because you're not trying to impress him," J supplied.

"You're showing him the free, straightforward, blunt-as-all-hell Liddy we see every day," Sam continued. "No man's heart stands a chance from falling when you show that side."

Jordan smacked Liddy's thigh and stood. "Okay, let's go pumpkin. The slopes are calling us."

Why does everyone love slapping my ass?

LIDDY LEANED INTO the skis, stretching her calf muscles and letting her ankle adjust. The first time since her injury, and finally back on the mountain. She grinned at the run ahead of her.

Finally.

Luke stood beside her. "You ready?"

"Born that way."

They skied next to each other down the first section. He was always a few arm lengths away, giving her space, but close enough to intervene if she had problems. After a short while, she was confident enough to try the next run by herself.

"I'll meet you up ahead in a bit."

"You sure?" he asked.

"Take a hike, clinger." She winked.

His million-dollar grin left her breathless as he said, "Sure thing, sweet cheeks."

He pushed off down the hill, picking up speed quickly.

Where did he get that gorgeous smile?

It pissed her off that she liked it so much, especially when his eyes twinkled at her. *All the girls probably get that same smile. Butthead.*

Her cell phone buzzed in her pocket.

She pulled it out, and smiled at the caller ID.

Nancy Hale, the Executive Director at Holly House.

She answered. "Good morning, Nan. Happy Thanksgiving."

"Same to you. Just calling to see how your vacation went."

"Well, I'm staring at the sweetest blue I've ever seen."

"Wait, I'm confused," Nancy replied. "You're not back yet?"

Liddy chuckled. "Long story. I get back in town tomorrow. How are things at my favorite non-profit?"

"Busy, as always. We've had two new adoptions finalized this week."

"Fantastic. This is normally the hardest time of the year for these kids. Well done, Nan."

"It hasn't been easy. June's retirement hasn't gone as smoothly as we'd hoped. Her replacement, Meadow, just found an entire cabinet full of paperwork June had put files in. Seems to be from before our electronic filing days."

Liddy winced. "Ouch. Anything you need help with?" June was a sweet old woman who'd been around back when Liddy was a kid in the foster system. She'd more than earned her retirement.

"I think we can handle it. So far, just lots of old invoices and home visit reports—but we're going cross-eyed. We really need to get those loaded to the electronic system."

She laughed and didn't envy the person scanning and uploading all those papers by hand.

"Anyway," Nancy continued. "We could use your help if

you have some time this weekend. Though, I'd hate to drag you away from your family."

"You know my parents won't mind. In fact, they'll come up and help too, if we ask them. I'll see you Saturday."

"Thanks, doll!"

She slipped her phone back into the inside pocket of her jacket and zipped it closed, then lowered her new goggles over her eyes.

What a glorious view. Sunlight beamed off the snow-covered evergreen forest that extended as far as her eyes could see. More mountain ranges stretched around her in every direction, and wispy clouds seemed to dance off the peaks. The pine trees narrowed the farther down the hill she looked. Off in the distance she noticed a small *hole* in the green blanket of trees. Sparks Pond sat like a dark blue watering trough for Mother Nature.

After letting a few skiers go ahead of her, she dug in her poles to push off and let gravity send her sailing. Jordan was right. The snowfall made the runs perfect.

She followed the signs down, everything clearly marked, and her mind wandered back to Luke. Her feelings were a jumbled mess when she thought about him.

He was gorgeous, but arrogant as shit. He was caring, but boisterous and egocentric. She couldn't for the life of her figure out why she liked him. He was a polar opposite of anyone she'd ever dated before.

Maybe because he awoke a new appetite inside her, one

she didn't even know she had. A thirst for the rawer kind of sex. More adventurous.

But her heart had flipped over when he'd asked to see her that night.

The wind in her face felt . . . freeing. This was really what she needed. A break from the monotony, from the rain, from boredom, from her life.

Okay, so what if she needed this break, *including* Luke, for a reason. Even for just a few days, she got to be relaxed and comfortable in her own skin for a while. Put the daily grind on hold.

Oh! Maybe grind isn't the word I should use.

She giggled to herself.

But that's what it was like sometimes. Day in and day out at the boutique, helping rich customers fill their closets with overpriced clothing and accessories. Granted, the designers were artists and everything was high quality, but at the end of the day it was just clothing. And a paycheck. Her real fulfillment had come through volunteering at Holly House. Because they *needed* her help. Some of their situations were so dire, so traumatic, people like those at the non-profit were sorely needed. Liddy lived for the days a child was officially adopted. But those moments were rare and few, with a lot of turmoil and agony in between.

She knew that fact, intimately.

Breaks were necessary for survival. To get away and remind her of the beauty in the world.

And this mountain was pretty damn beautiful to her. Not to mention a cocky, hot-as-hellfire ski instructor.

She skidded to the bottom of the run, ready to do it all again.

Chapter TWELVE

LUKE STOOD BY the threshold of the Lodge's main ballroom, where a massive table had been completely decked out for Thanksgiving dinner for all the guests, along with all the resort staff. Family style.

Because that's the way the resort treated everyone, like family.

He grinned at the stellar setup. Lit candles running down the center interspersed with dishes of yams, green beans, cranberries, mashed potatoes, and several oven-roasted turkeys, covered with gleaming silver cloches to keep them warm. More home-cooked food than could possibly be consumed in one sitting. Every year seemed to get bigger than the previous one.

His phone buzzed, and he pulled it from his pocket. The screen displayed his mother's beautiful face.

"Happy Thanksgiving," he answered.

"And to you, darling. What are you doing?"

"About to sit down to a delicious meal at the resort.

What about you?"

"We just finished. It's late here, but I wanted to talk to you before we retired for the night."

"Did Chloe or Samuel's family make it?"

"Chloe left an hour ago. Samuel and Karina spent this week with her family. They'll be here for Christmas—because they found out that's when *you'll* be home."

Luke smiled. "Great. Can't wait to see them. It's good to hear your voice."

"Chloe told me to wish you a happy Thanksgiving."

Of course she did. She probably left out the kick in the shins to go with it. "She called me the other day."

"Did she?"

"You already know what she talked to me about."

"No, can't say I do."

"Mom, I love you. But there's nothing wrong in asking for help. If that's what you need."

"Does that mean you'll do it? If I ask you, will you come back and take over the foundation?"

Luke tightened his grip on the phone. He hated this part. He didn't want his family to use this as an excuse to get him to move back. Hearing his mother struggling to keep her precious foundation going stung his insides, but what if this was just a ploy to manipulate him into doing something he didn't really want to do?

"I told Chloe I'd think about it. But I want you to understand that if I say no, that doesn't mean you should continue to overwork yourself. If you need help, get it. The replacement doesn't have to be me."

She sighed. "I think that's the closest I've gotten you to consider moving home in ten years."

He almost chuckled. "You must've caught me on a good day."

"You sound different. Rather happy."

He stared across the space, realizing his mother was right. "I am."

"How much have you had to drink?"

He snorted. "Nothing, yet."

The pause on the other end of the phone brought up his guard. "I know that voice. You've met someone."

"Why would you jump to that conclusion?"

"Because I know my children very well. What's her name? What's she like?"

Just as his mother asked the question, Liddy walked into the room. Her long locks clipped back on the sides, and in this dim lighting held a honey glow. Her angora cowl neck sweater matched the pink in her leggings, and of course, cream socks poked out of brown leather hiking boots.

The woman of his dreams.

The second her gaze found his, her grin nearly knocked him off his feet.

Heat rose on his cheeks, because *damn*. "I'll tell you everything later, Mom. The dinner bell is ringing."

"Fine, leave me hanging. I'm only your mother."

"Love you."

"Love you, too."

They hung up.

Luke strolled down one side of the long table, watching Liddy as she walked in the same direction on the other side— her gaze glued to his. He was absently aware her friends followed behind her. It didn't matter where he sat, just as long as he was beside her.

When they finally met at the end of the table, he leaned in to kiss her cheek. Her orange and lavender scent combined into a heady fragrance he wanted to lick off her skin, right then and there. "You look lovely."

"Thanks. So do you."

Luke reached to shake Jordan's hand. "You ladies have fun today?"

The brunette shook her head. "We Californians hug." She pulled him in for a one-armed squeeze. "Vacations are always a blast. Thanks for taking such *great care* of our Liddy." She winked at him as she pulled away.

He would've blushed, if he weren't so damn mesmerized by the blonde that filled his dreams.

Liddy was a fireball, and she had fireball friends.

Luke dropped his head to hide his smile.

Chapter THIRTEEN

HAS ANYONE SEEN my brown hiking boots?" Sam called from the living room.

"Why is it every trip we take, someone can't find their shoes? Try in the closet," Jordan replied.

"Oh, yippee. This is gonna be so much fun."

"You sound like you've never been to a bonfire before," Liddy said.

"I haven't." Sam shoved her foot into the boot.

"Oh, brother," Jordan said in a stage whisper.

But none of the women could hold back their laughter.

After several hours of skiing and a hearty Thanksgiving dinner for fifty, Luke had reminded them of the resort's post-meal bonfire at the top of the hill. He'd smiled at all of them, and threaded his fingers in Liddy's. He brought up her hand to kiss her knuckles.

"Liddy knows the way," he'd explained with a sly smile as he walked away from the dinner spread.

The girls had given her a good-natured ribbing for that.

But something about Luke, under the stars again, sent her heart racing.

"Okay, everybody got everything?" Jordan's voice rang out.

"I think so," Sam replied as she grabbed her hat off the counter.

"I'm still full," Liddy announced.

"Well, you're gonna have to work it off," Jordan said with a grin.

The three zipped up their jackets and headed to the promise of warmth, and some extra heat for her.

LUKE COULDN'T MISS the smiling face on Liddy, on all three of them, as they made it to the clearing. Several staff members had prepped the area and started the fire while the guests finished dinner. The resort hosted a bonfire every Thanksgiving, Christmas, and New Year's for those that stayed over the holidays, and it was always a hit.

"Good evening, ladies."

"Evening, Luke," they spoke in unison.

He had to grin. "I saved you all a spot over on this bench. You'll be nice and warm here, out of the smoke plume."

As they took a seat, Bryan, the general manager, caught everyone's attention with a whistle. "Evening, folks. I'm glad you're here at the Buffalo Ridge Resort this Thanksgiving. How was dinner? Didn't our chef do an incredible job?"

People smiled and applauded the chef.

"I've met some of you, but for those that I haven't, I'm Bryan Shaw. I'm glad you chose to spend your holiday with us, and I hope you will consider joining us again. Now, before we get started with the games, and the s'mores, if you have room . . ." Several people chuckled. "I'd like to share that we at the resort, including the owners, take our job of stewardship for the planet seriously. You may have noticed the low-flow faucets, showerheads, and toilets. We also compost all the kitchen scraps. All the light switches in the Lodge are on automatic sensors. And I'm sure you've all seen the recycling bins around, and have been using them. Hint hint. These are just a few things. The website has the entire list. So, please enjoy the bonfire guilt-free." He smiled and gave a brief wave while the audience applauded him again.

"Okay, folks," Stephanie, the front desk manager, began, "Our first game is Name That Tune. Steven, here, will play the first few bars of a song, and you all have to guess the title. Then we sing that song before moving on."

This one's always a crowd-pleaser.

Luke knew all the songs, after ten years at the resort, but sometimes, Steven threw in a curve ball. His boss turned up the volume on the wireless speakers to "Respect," by Aretha Franklin. Most everyone knew that song, and easily sang along.

Luke leaned in and took Liddy's hand. She looked over and smiled. Gently, he pulled her to standing, and brought her in front of him.

"How's the ankle?" he murmured low in her ear.

"One-hundred percent."

"Good to hear." He rested his hands on her shoulders while Steven played "Sweet Caroline," by Neil Diamond. Another crowd-pleaser.

He started massaging her shoulders discreetly. He loved having his hands on her, but he also wanted her thinking about spending the night with him. The idea had swum around in his mind all freakin' day, not just because of the amazing hot monkey-sex. He could not get the woman out of his head. He'd have to figure out a way to see her again after she left.

Next, Steven played "Brown Eyed Girl," by Van Morrison. She turned her head and whispered, "I love this song."

He sang a few lines in her ear, and slid a hand to her hip, over the snug jeans she wore. He caressed down and pulled up over her ass. He couldn't wait to peel those things off.

She leaned her backside into him, that gorgeous ass skimming his growing erection. The smell of her filled his senses.

When the song ended and everyone cheered, Steven queued the next song.

"How about we get out of here?"

She nodded.

"Meet you on the path." He released her, instantly missing the warmth of her body.

He slowly stepped away and watched her return to her friends on the bench. They leaned forward to hear her talk.

Luke walked away from the clearing and down the path several feet, and waited out of the group's line of sight. The anticipation to be with a woman had never been so great. But Liddy wasn't just some woman he'd picked up at a bar. She had a vulnerability to her, an honesty and realism that he rarely found in others. Once again, he considered telling her the full truth—that he was a Rothchild.

In his gut, he believed he could trust her.

Up to this point, all his relationships were kept at arm's length, and for a very good reason. People loved money before they loved people.

Call him a cynic, he didn't care. People gravitated toward money before even learning about the person. If they did learn about the money, everything changed. Never in a good way.

He couldn't go through life wondering if it was him or the cash.

He had nothing against the money. Money didn't buy happiness, but it bought choices. For that, he was grateful.

Liddy strolled down the path, the sight of her white coat and cheery face pulling him from his thoughts. She was gorgeous, even in the dark.

She stood before him and smiled. "Ready?"

He cupped his hands over the sides of her head and brought her precious lips to his.

She opened for him, willing and adventurous.

"I want you so badly," he muttered, "I could take you behind those trees. Yank those jeans off that delectable body, and have you screaming my name over and over."

She licked her lips, her hazel eyes darkening. "Egomaniac. I'd scream my own name."

He grinned. She was feisty, and he fucking couldn't get enough. "We'll see."

He laced his fingers through hers and led her down the mountain to the employees' quarters. The separate dormitory for resort staff was a miniature version of the Lodge on the outside, quaint log-cabin style with warm lighting around the whole structure. Almost like a cottage.

"You don't seem overly concerned about people seeing us together." Liddy pulled tighter into his shoulder. Either from the cold or nerves he couldn't say.

"No. People rarely have *relations* here. The owners don't encourage it, obviously, but there's no written rule against it." He'd checked on that the first day she'd arrived. "Basically, I don't suspect anyone will care."

"I hope not."

They walked through the door into the common area. The living room lights switched on, revealing empty suede couches and a black, flat-screen television over the stone fireplace.

"Cozy," she said.

"Everyone's still at the bonfire or working at the Lodge. So, we have this whole residence to ourselves for a while.

Kitchen is well stocked during the season, when most of the employees are here, as you can see."

He was thankful the kitchen counters were cleared off, leaving just the butcher's block and coffee machine on stainless steel tops. A miracle, considering it was Patrick's day for kitchen duty.

"Where's your room?" Liddy's gaze nearly dazzled. Clearly, anticipating the night ahead.

"Down the hall." He kissed her knuckles.

Then, with her hand in his, he led her down the quiet hall, passing closed doors. He opened the door to his room, watching her scan the place when he flipped on the light.

"You're quite tidy," she said as she walked around, glancing at his pictures, his desk, and his bed.

Gave it a thorough cleaning this morning.

He reached for one of the candles on the top of his chest of drawers, and used his lighter to light it.

As he moved to the second candle, Liddy's hands smoothed over his thigh—then up along his ass, working to his torso.

It was all he could do to concentrate on not burning his fingers lighting the next candle.

LIDDY DIDN'T KNOW when she became so bold, but seeing Luke's fine ass made her want to grab it.

Maybe Sam was right. This was her true nature: *the free, straightforward, blunt-as-all-hell Liddy we see every day.*

He moved to turn around.

She grabbed his shoulders to keep him still. "Don't move."

"Yes, ma'am."

Her hands roamed free. She didn't need to see a damn thing to know a strong chiseled chest from sculpted abs from a rock-hard cock. He took great care of his body. By the feel of him, skiing wasn't his only exercise.

She yanked off his jacket, then with his help, his long-sleeve shirt. What a fine model of the male species. And his woodsy smell was intoxicating.

She slid her hands to his jeans and unfastened them, surprised at how effortless it was for her. She wasted no time reaching in for her prize. Her hand wrapped around him.

The groan from his lips made her feel empowered.

She stroked him slowly up and down.

His head fell between his arms, still perched on the highboy.

"I've been thinking about you all day," she admitted in his ear. "Waiting for the next time we have wild, hot, monkey-sex. The kind where we have space, and can move around."

He turned his face toward her, the corner of his mouth lifted, revealing a delectable dimple. "Hot monkey-sex? There's a new one I'm thrilled to try."

Her thumb smoothed the precum from the tip down and around. She gently stroked, loving the silky feel of him in her hands.

He groaned again. "Sweet cheeks, I'm 'bout to make a big mess here if you don't stop."

She released him. "Making messes is what we're good at. Turn around."

When he complied, she whipped off her jacket and dropped to her knees. She caught the surprise in his eyes just before she took him in her mouth.

"Fuck, Liddy. You have an amazing mouth." His fingers tangled in her hair. "Christ."

She took him deep, as far as she could without gagging, and sucked hard on the way up.

He growled. "Angel, you have to stop."

No way. He was young. He could recharge quickly.

She fisted him just a bit more snugly and worked him until she felt his release in her mouth. She drank him down, every last drop, as he groaned and panted and pulled on her hair.

He rested his hands on her shoulders, regaining his breath and just stared down at her in awe.

"My fine woman . . ." Oh, that had a nice ring to her ears. "Strip."

She rose, and, with his help, the clothes went flying. His too.

He pulled, crashing her naked body to his, and his demanding lips to hers.

She gasped. Then she snaked her arms around his neck, pushing her body against him, adoring the skin to skin contact.

With his arm tucked tight around her waist, he backed her into the bed. She sank down and scooched herself to the center.

He climbed over her, giving her a quick peck on the lips. "Aren't you a clever one?" His gorgeous eyes a deep blue sapphire, brimmed with desire.

"Me?"

His finger stroked up her wet center.

"Unh." She ached for his touch. From the moment he'd laid his hands on her shoulders at the bonfire and whispered in her ear, she'd been ready.

He gently pushed in one finger, teasing her with the lack of depth.

"Luke," she begged.

Another finger entered her, tempting her in the same manner. He knew he was driving her insane.

Then with no more torment, he slammed into her completely, catching her cry in his mouth. His fingers worked her, turning, twisting, stroking her core.

She moaned ceaselessly, her arms reached overhead, for what, she had no idea. She broke the kiss to pant. "Luke," she cried out. Any more, she thought she might explode. The intensity grew.

He lowered his body between her legs. She watched him give her one last look before he claimed her clit with his mouth.

"Ah!" she cried. Her back bowed off the bed.

His tongue spun over her clit, pushing and lapping while his fingers played in the slip-slide.

She writhed and couldn't hold back any longer.

He laid his free arm across her tummy, grounding her, as the delicious torture continued, bringing her to an unfathomable orgasm. So powerful she thought she might pass out.

He released her, pulling out his fingers, and lay flush beside her.

Her racing heart slowly subsided.

"Angel, you are beautiful when you come."

She reached for him, pulling his mouth to her, tasting herself in the kiss.

He pulled back long enough to grab a condom and sheath himself. He lay down at her side and her leg rested on his hip. Facing each other, he carefully pushed into her wet channel.

His top leg bent, bringing them closer in the joining.

"God, you feel amazing."

"So do you."

They moved in sync, making their own beautiful music. For the first time, Liddy didn't want to leave this narcissist. She wanted more than just this vacation.

"Liddy."

She peeled her eyes away from his lips to look into his deep blue eyes.

"We can keep this going."

She stared, thinking about how a long-distance thing would work.

"I can come see you during off-season. I have a lot of time off."

She grinned. "Yeah?"

He pushed her onto her back, still moving slowly with her. "I don't want to see anyone else. I know you hate me—"

"I do," she panted through a grin. *I hate him in all the right ways.*

He chuckled. "But we have a lot in common."

"Like what?"

He thrust in, making her gasp. "We both love *this*, for one." He groaned, caressing her neck through another plunge.

"That doesn't count." Liddy bit her lip, reveling in how deep he was. "It has to be . . . more than physical." *I won't make the mistake again of equating lust with love.*

"We love skiing," he continued. "We want to be independent and free of other's expectations, but still appreciated for who we are. To share our lives with someone with the same thirst for life. And you definitely have an insatiable thirst. Or should I say a healthy *appetite.*" He moved deep inside her again, making her grip onto his waist tighter.

He makes a really good point. "Thank God for that."

"You call me out on my shit, and give it back to me just as much. That, and . . ." he covered her lips with his mouth, devouring her breath. As if this were his Thanksgiving meal, and he'd not eaten for weeks.

The whiskey on his tongue from the bonfire was oaky and rich. She could taste him for hours, getting drunk off him.

"So fucking delicious." He licked his lips. "You are completely irresistible. Damn, I *really* like you."

"You do?"

He traced his finger along her chin. "Whadya say?"

What do I say? Her heart told her to jump in with both feet, no question. But her mind pulled on the reins, reminding her of her previous clingy behavior. She had a history of leaping without looking, and this time she wanted to know exactly what she was getting into.

Intuition told her she and Luke were equals in this relationship. The same fears, the same intensity, the same hopes. Perhaps both knowing they had to trust each other, because they each had something to lose . . .

Just maybe.

"Okay. Let's see where this goes."

His smile was big and brilliant, and she knew, sincere. He wanted to be with her. And she felt the same. The thought of never seeing Luke again hurt her heart. She didn't know how to make a thousand-mile-relationship work, but it was worth a try. She owed it to herself.

He dove into her, pushing her closer to climax. He took her parted lips, swallowing her gasps as they both climbed toward a blissful finish together.

She broke away, and screamed out his name.

He groaned into the crux of her shoulder and bit down gently.

Gees! She could definitely have more of this arrogant, cocky man in her life.

They rested for a moment, when he rolled to the side, staring in her eyes. "You're beautiful."

"Thank you," she whispered back.

"Give me a minute. I'll bring you a washcloth, okay?"

She nodded.

As he went to the bathroom, she rose and immediately went to the mirror above the desk. Pushing her hair out of the way, she had to see how big the bite mark was that he left. She grinned. Not that she cared too much. Every vacation required a souvenir.

Absently, she glanced down and saw his stack of mail. The name on the top envelope was odd. Addressed to Luke Sawyer Rothchild.

Rothchild?

She stared a bit longer. It's probably not *the* Rothchild family. The one the whole country knew about, and the media couldn't stop reporting on. That family's fame was on a whole other playing field, above even the clients of her high-end boutique.

She brushed it off, but the knot in her stomach was already there.

Luke returned and smiled. "Lay down, sweet cheeks."

She glanced at the naked, sculpted Adonis with strong shoulders and muscular chest with a smattering of hair. Breathtaking. The man held a washcloth, ready to clean every inch of her.

Oh my.

She scooted to the center of the bed when he pushed her legs farther apart to run a warm cloth over her.

"Mmm."

"You like that?"

She moaned and in no time, she'd forgotten about the letter on his desk. No time to think about nonsensical stuff like that when a gorgeous man hovered over wanting nothing more than to hear her scream his name. Again.

FOURTEEN

LIDDY TYPED LUKE'S name into the search engine, not sure why she was holding her breath.

Back at her own cabin, she shifted on the barstool, deliciously sore from the hours of lovemaking with Luke. She prayed the last name was purely coincidental. She couldn't tell Sam and Jordan about what she'd seen. Not until she knew for sure.

She clicked, trying to be as quiet as possible so she wouldn't wake the girls. A few links came back, with photos of Luke, and his family.

The Rothchild family.

Liddy tried to take a full breath.

A beautiful, pristinely manicured grouping of people in front of some charity ribbon-cutting ceremony. His brother and sister looked just like him, all three mirroring either their mother's statuesque smile or their father's severe eyes.

Speaking of his father, that was one extremely expensive silk suit he wore, and an even pricier gold watch. His mother wore a fancy designer skirt suit Liddy recognized from the shop. In fact, the whole family's wardrobe in that picture surpassed a year's earnings.

Luke stood beside his sister, handsome and dapper in a Brooks Brothers suit and tie. But his smile wasn't real. Almost like he tried to emulate the stuffy exterior of his father.

Almost like he wasn't happy.

So, what was he doing out in Colorado as a ski-bum instructor, if that kind of massive fortune waited for him back home?

She found a video interview with Luke's mother, Meredith. The interviewer congratulated her on her eldest son's marriage to the daughter of another tycoon family. The thirty-something interviewer went on about the Rothchild Foundation. From what Liddy could gather, Luke's mom was the president of the foundation, and their annual fundraiser was coming up.

"Can we expect another fabulous event?"

"Absolutely. Tickets are already sold out," his mother began, in a designer blouse and skirt set, her three-strand pearl necklace accentuating her perfect skin. *"Next year will likely surpass this year's. For the most exciting news, I'm at liberty to share that Celine Dion will grace us with her glorious voice."*

"Celine? Wow! That's quite a coup."

"Indeed." Her smile was brilliant white and perfect. *"Exactly what people have come to expect with the Rothchild*

name—upholding the highest standards of excellence."

Oh God. Liddy swallowed the lump in her throat. She barely heard the rest of the interview.

Even if Luke did *sort of* like her, there was no way his parents would approve of her. The proof was before her, on replay with her HD screen. How could she compare, or dream of measuring up?

After a few more clicks, Liddy came across a business insider page, where they'd estimated the Rothchild family fortune. The number nearly made her throw up—there was an absurd number of zeros behind the dollar sign.

She closed the browser, then shut her laptop, her hands cupped over her mouth. Liddy stared at the log cabin wall for several minutes, trying desperately to quell the rancid feeling in her chest.

Holy shitballs.

He'd lied to her. About who he was.

Even had the audacity to try and continue their *relationship* under the same false pretenses.

Her heart cleaved with every beat.

She wasn't even good enough for him to bother using his real name. Trying to *slum* it incognito.

Liddy shoved herself away from the desk and escaped into the bathroom to wash her hands.

Then her face.

She felt so dirty.

She stripped her clothes to get in the shower and wash

him off.

All of him.

She turned on the faucet, and waited for it to warm.

In the mirror, she focused on the small scars by her collarbone and the dark circles under her eyes.

Even if Luke hadn't used a false name, there was no way someone like her could've fit into the same world as the Rothchilds.

She'd only be counting the days—or hours—until he'd cast her aside. Just like her childhood.

Never wanted. Charity case turned liability.

Why do I even care? No point in being angry over a vacation romance. Like there had ever been a chance at anything permanent.

"You weren't supposed to be looking anyway, Lid," she chided herself.

That was the angriest shower in her life. But after, she still felt too dirty—and enraged—to sleep.

She scoured her room, packing all her things to leave the next day. Hours ahead of schedule, but there was no reason to linger.

We can keep this going. She scoffed at the words he'd cooed in her ear.

The nerve of him.

Only in your worst nightmares, ass cheeks.

AT FIRST LIGHT, Liddy burst through his dormitory door, knocking it against the wall.

"Luke Sawyer!"

He sat up like a rocket, his eyes red from lack of sleep. He'd only had about three hours after their late-night tryst.

"What? What's wrong?" He squinted at the clock. "What time is it?"

"Time for all liars to come clean."

He scraped the back of his neck. "What are you talking about?"

She grabbed the piece of mail from his dresser, the one with his *full* name, and flung it at him. "You're a *Rothchild*. Where the hell do you come off trying to lie to me?"

"I never lied." He peeled the covers off, and stood bare-chested in front of her. *Damn.* The man was distracting. Even his morning-after hair, messy and wild, was damn sexy. He stared at the letter. "How did you see this?" he finally asked.

She pointed to the stack of mail on his dresser, her finger stabbing through the air like an accuser at the culprit of deceit and fraud. "I'm not a snoop. You left it out on your desk. How come you didn't tell me?"

"Does it matter?" he asked.

"Of course, it does. Otherwise, you wouldn't go by Sawyer."

"Because I didn't want people to like me for money or my name." He tossed the mail on the bed. "I wanted them to like me for me. Is that so difficult to understand?" All humor had vanished from his face leaving him vulnerable, but she could see him building up his defenses.

She bit her tongue as images of their brief week together flashed fresh and vivid. She'd actually felt alive, until now…

"I grew up around people who valued money more than relationships," he continued. "Who judged *my* value based on my last name. Most of my friendships, and the woman I thought was the love of my life, were all fake. But here," he held out his arms and gestured to the resort. "They like me for me. Or at least they did, until now."

Liddy glanced behind her at the open door, where someone peered in.

"Everything okay in here?" another instructor asked.

"Give us a minute, Patrick." Luke pulled on a Buffalo T-shirt, and scraped his hands through his hair again.

"You know," Liddy cleared her throat over the lump lodged there. "The tragic thing is that I *did* like you for you. Because I thought you liked me for me. After that whole conversation about trust, and how hard it is for each of us." *Damn, my shaking voice.* "Come to find out, you were just slumming it with me. I'm not even good enough to know your real name. That's one of the most disrespectful things I've ever seen. And boy, have I seen some shit."

His eyes widened. He stepped forward. "I never meant—"

Liddy stepped back. "It doesn't matter anyway. Because I can't relate to *your* world. *My* world is a just a little too rugged and real for the *ultimate American family*." He probably planned to treat her as his plaything until his family met her, learned of her less-than-lustrous childhood, and then he'd cast her aside. That kind of rejection would be far too catastrophic to take.

Best to cut it off. Eventually, he'd leave. No one stayed forever. "We were just temporary anyway."

Luke stumbled forward, his eyes wide in shock.

Tears threatened to fall, and she couldn't bear the thought of crying in front of him. Liddy turned on her heel and rushed out, ignoring the slight ache in her ankle. The damn thing could break, for all she cared—just so long as she got the hell out of this place.

Chapter FIFTEEN

LUKE IGNORED EVERYONE'S stares as he strolled into the kitchen. After a shower and fresh clothes, he'd finally emerged from his room in desperate need of coffee. Several other resort employees sat at the island eating breakfast or checking the weather forecast.

He shoved his hands in his jeans pockets, fully expecting people to either turn their backs because they thought he'd lied all this time, or to start clamoring over him with questions about his family.

He'd managed to go nearly ten years without his last name divulged. Without his co-workers knowing he was an heir to an obnoxious fortune. A few people looked up at him before going back to their food.

Patrick set down his fork. "You all right?"

He nodded.

"There's biscuits left, and some gravy. Grab a plate."

Luke stared at him. "You don't have anything to say?"

Patrick looked confused. "About what? That you're a

Rothchild?"

He pursed his lips. "Yeah."

His friend scoffed and shoved another bite in his mouth. "Quick, grab the camera. Get a picture of the rich, fancy, yuppie who can't ski for shit."

A couple folks snickered.

Luke smirked. "At least I can make it down Devil's Crotch in twenty minutes. Your fastest was, what, twenty-eight?"

Patrick smiled. "Sawyer or Rothchild, same jackass, different day. You're still gonna cover your shifts, right?"

He crossed his arms. "I'm no slacker."

Patrick grimaced. "Debatable." Then he smiled.

A huge weight lifted off Luke's shoulders. He poured himself an orange juice.

"Tonight's first round is on Luke," Patrick quipped behind him.

Everyone laughed.

Luke loaded up a plate, but didn't really have an appetite. Not now. His friends at the resort may have been fine with this new revelation, but his mind went back to Liddy.

He'd considered moving to San Francisco to be with Liddy. The more he'd thought about it overnight, the more he loved the idea. Seemed infinitely more appealing than returning to New York to run his mother's foundation. He loved his family, but he knew where that path led—the kinds of people he'd have to manage and suffer through. But with

Liddy, the path was wide open. New possibilities to forge in a place he didn't know, with people who didn't know him.

Damn, how exciting that would've been.

He stabbed his food and shoved a bite into his mouth. One of his favorite breakfasts now tasted like ash.

"There's plenty more stars in the sky," Patrick muttered next to him. "Start wishing on another one."

Luke scowled. "Is that your version of lots more fish in the sea?"

Patrick shrugged. "I'm just sayin', she ain't the only blonde, eight-plus to come through here. Don't get so down in the dumps."

"What happens when you come across a twelve, who actually likes you back?"

"Did she?"

Luke bit his tongue. He thought she did. Actually, she'd hated him, but loved screwing him. When he'd brought up the idea of taking it further, she'd actually smiled. One so big, so beautiful, how else was he supposed to interpret that?

She'd liked him, a lot.

And he had to go and screw that up, even if it was unintentional.

"I CAN'T BELIEVE it," Jordan gawked when Liddy explained what she'd discovered about Luke. "That's an *insane* fortune behind him. And he's out here being a ski instructor?"

Sam's expression was a little more discerning, but she remained silent.

Liddy held onto the seat in the shuttle on the way to the airport. The roads were a little sketchy after a recent snowfall and a drop in temperature, although the driver didn't appear too concerned.

"I don't care about the money," Liddy replied. "He lied to me. Didn't even show me the courtesy of giving his real name. How I can even *think* about a relationship with someone like that?"

"He said he wanted to take the relationship beyond this week?" Jordan asked. "Really?"

Liddy tightened her hold on the cushion, remembering the mind-shattering orgasm he'd given her, just after he'd asked to keep their relationship going long-distance. *Because I really like you.* "His words and actions don't match."

Sam opened her mouth, but stopped, then sat back against the seat, not meeting Liddy's gaze.

"What?" Liddy asked.

Her friend pressed her lips together. "I agree, lying to someone you have strong feelings for is never the right choice, but I can also see why he did it."

Now, it was Liddy's turn to gawk. "You're taking *his* side?"

"I'm always on your side. But imagine living your life surrounded by people with hidden agendas. Who always wanted something from you, even something as simple as shaking your hand for a photo op. Wouldn't you be a little more guarded about who you let into your life?"

Liddy blinked. She'd been too focused on the pain from his deception, instead of trying to understand the *why* from his side. Her life hadn't been easy either, always wondering who she could trust not to reject her. *That* part she could understand.

"In the end, it doesn't matter anyway." Liddy cleared her throat. "After seeing the interview from his family, who are so focused on exceptional talents and *upholding the highest standards*, there's no way they would ever accept me. My past of no solid foundation, of multiple broken homes, automatically disqualifies me."

Sam's brow furrowed. "What are you talking about? What interview?"

Liddy pulled out her phone and showed them the video she found of his mother.

"See, 'upholding the highest standards of excellence.' Meaning, the Rothchilds only accept the most exceptional. Someone from a freakin' dynasty or at least a decent pedigree. How am I supposed to compete with that?"

Jordan looked at her sideways. "I'm not sure that's what she meant."

"What do you mean? It pretty clear to me." She ached all over again, just listening and staring at the screen. For the briefest moment in Liddy's history, she'd thought, this could be it. He may be the one.

"First of all," Sam cut in. "This is only a clip of the interview, not the whole thing, so there's a lot of context missing. Secondly, I think she's talking in a business sense, about the foundation. Not necessarily a list of requirements to join their family. You might be reading too much into that."

Her defenses instantly swirled to the surface, and her stomach clenched. If there was one thing Liddy had learned during her years in foster care, it was how to read parents. This Meredith woman screamed pretentious. She was cultured and polished, and knew how to act in the spotlight. No one was going to tarnish that image.

"Furthermore," Sam continued, her voice louder. "Who says you have to compete with anyone? It's about you and him, no one else."

Liddy shook her head. "Eventually, he'd leave anyway. They all leave. No one sticks around."

Sam grabbed her hand. "We do. We stick."

Tears pricked her eyes.

"Besides, they would be *crazy* not to love you, gajillionaires or not. Everything you've done, *despite* your childhood . . . you're like Wonder Woman. They'd be the luckiest family on the planet to have you as a daughter-in-law. The real question is, are they good enough for *you?*"

Liddy squeezed Sam's hand tight, the tears spilling over the brim. Even at her worst, these women still saw the virtue in her. "What in the world did I ever do to deserve you two?

Best friends a girl could ever hope for."

The flight home might as well have taken a century. Liddy kept her sunglasses on the whole time. Never mind it was night or that she was on a plane. Keeping the falling tears hidden or at least hiding her eyes because she looked like hell was her concern.

Sam leaned into her from the seat beside her. "We land in thirty minutes. Are you sure you don't want to stop for dinner on the way home? You haven't eaten a thing all day."

She shook her head. "I just want to unpack and go to bed."

Her friend frowned. "Okay. Maybe you should take the weekend off. Give yourself a little more time to . . . recuperate."

Liddy downed the rest of her vodka rocks. The liquor burnt going down her throat, but at least it helped distract her from the pain in her chest. Her splintered heart.

"I'm helping out at Holly House tomorrow. But I have to go back to work on Sunday. Need the extra shift to help pay for the absurd medical bills I'm going to get from my sprain."

"Jordan and I want to help cover those. It could have been any one of us that fell."

She took her sunglasses off, and looked her friend dead in the eyes. "Absolutely not. It wasn't your fault at all. It was an accident. Plus, I always pay my own way. You're a sweetheart to offer, but no. This is my responsibility."

Sam squeezed her hand, and didn't let go. The silence

between them filled up with the rushing jet engine, and the internal fog of her own misery.

Every mile they flew farther away from Luke weighed her heart a little more, but yet wasn't nearly enough distance. The sooner she put the man behind her, the better.

Even when she wasn't interested in finding a man, her heart still got broken.

But she knew what she had to do. She had to focus on work. Put all her energy in filling her days with shifts, and the rest of the time with volunteering at Holly House.

That would be her purpose. Nothing glamorous or high-profile, but still worthy.

Chapter SIXTEEN

LIDDY WALKED INTO Holly House first thing Saturday morning, ignoring the fact that her heart was still irreparably cracked.

The historic building was nearly deserted, which was unusual even for a Saturday. The receptionist's desk sat empty, the phone blinking with unheard voicemails. A half-consumed coffee mug waited unfinished, with papers strewn all over the top and the surrounding floor.

"Nancy?" Liddy asked hesitantly.

No one came around the corner.

Liddy helped herself to the back offices. Even though she technically didn't work at Holly House, she knew this building better than most of the current staff. She'd essentially grown up here, which is why she kept coming back to help out whenever they'd let her. The walls were still adorned with the framed photos of every single child they'd placed over the years. Hers hung beside the Executive Director's office door.

The desks on either side of the aisle were all empty, the

lights switched off. The only light on was from Nancy's office at the end of the hall where a few muddled voices came through, tense and on edge.

Liddy slowly approached, and peered inside, simultaneously rapping a single knuckle on the door.

Nancy looked up from her desk, her grayish-blonde bun undone from where she'd scraped her nails. Her reading glasses perched on the end of her nose, which had always reminded Liddy of an old-school librarian, but this time the chain they were normally attached to was missing.

Papers were scattered all over the tabletop. More stacked books sat open on the coffee table by the door. With a panicked expression, Maureen, the Assistant Director, scanned a few books on the same upholstered couch that Liddy had sat on countless times as a child after getting in trouble at a foster house. Maureen's jeans and loose-fitted brown sweater betrayed the normal business-casual atmosphere of the office. Which meant something was seriously wrong.

"What's going on? What can I do?" Liddy set down her purse just inside the door.

"We're panicking, obviously," Nancy replied, with a grimace.

"I can see that. Why?"

"Our certification is expired," Maureen interjected bluntly. "We never filed for a renewal. June just shoved the notice in her desk and forgot to tell anyone."

"Okay." Liddy kept her voice calm, knowing that adding to the panic would only make things worse. "We can fix that."

"You don't understand. We have to shut down until the renewal is approved. Which means the adoptions we finalized this week can't go through."

"They'll go through," Liddy assured, even though she had no idea if that was true. But, dammit, they'd figure it out. "We just need to send in the renewal today. I'll walk it over to the courthouse myself."

"If it were that easy, don't you think I would've done it myself by now?" Nancy snapped. She bit her lip. "I'm sorry. I'm not angry with you." She removed her reading glasses and tossed them on the desk. "But the certification requirements have changed. They now apparently require additional documentation we don't have, and filings have to be done by an attorney. Of which ours is out on vacation right now, along with every other attorney in their office. Since the certification is already expired, we have to jump through a thousand other hoops that will take forever." Her voice hitched. "And I can't bear the thought of those kids . . . those families . . . hearing this."

Liddy knew how important this place was to Nancy, and to every single person who worked here. Holly House meant infinitely *more* to the children and families they served. No one understood that like Liddy herself.

"You won't have to inform them of anything, Nan." She rolled up her sleeves, and dug her phone out of her purse. "I'm going to order lunch for us, so we can have some fuel while we work. Keep digging for the documents we need. I'm going to call every single attorney I know, even if that means scouring all of San Francisco and San Mateo counties."

After two hours, and a bazillion phone calls, Liddy reached one indubitable conclusion—law offices weren't open on Saturday.

"Crap," she said under her breath.

She entered June's old office.

Nancy looked up. "I think we've got most of it." Her eyes narrowed. "Maureen, I think the insurance policy is kept in the front filing cabinet. Would you go get it?" She glanced at the list of required documentation. "It's unrealistic to think that a nonprofit would keep every document it generates," Nancy told anyone listening.

"Nancy." She looked up from the mass of papers in front of her. "I couldn't get a hold of a law office. No one is open on Saturday."

God, she felt so defeated.

Nancy's body slumped. "Oh, God. It has to be done this weekend. Filed by Sunday at midnight. Monday is too late." She dropped into the office chair behind her.

"I left messages. We might still get a call-back. Let's keep getting everything together."

The phone rang, and from the sound of it, Maureen picked it up in the front office. *Oh, praise Jesus.*

"I'm going to see who that is. Be right back." *Hopefully*

with good news.

"Thank you, sir. I appreciate it." Maureen hung up the phone.

"Who was that?" Liddy asked.

"Someone wanting to make a donation. I asked him to call back Monday."

"He didn't happen to be an attorney, did he?"

Maureen chuckled, mostly to release the stress of the day. "No, I don't think so."

"If any of those law firms call back, let me know. I've left about a dozen messages all over San Francisco."

"Of course." She waved a folder in the air with glee. "Found the insurance file. One step closer."

They both hustled back to June's old office and added the papers to the pile. "Got it."

"Great." Nancy scanned the list. "I think we just need donor records, and that's easy to print out." She looked up. "Now, we need this form notarized, and an attorney to call back that knows non-profit and can file on our behalf to ensure compliance."

Liddy swallowed, her throat parched. Her hands were covered in ink and grime from all the papers they'd searched through—not to mention about a dozen paper cuts.

"We have to keep trying," she sighed. "These kids *need* us to fix this."

She glanced at the clock on the wall, the hour hand drawing way too close to five o'clock.

AFTER LIDDY HAD left the way she did, he'd resigned himself to accepting that they had no hope, no future. But damn, he wanted to do something for her. Make up for any slight he may have done.

He still had Jordan and Sam's cell numbers from when Liddy had sprained her ankle, so he called Jordan, for starters.

"Jordan, it's Luke."

"Whoa. Hi. What's up?" The hesitancy in her voice made him nervous.

"Look, I want to make a donation to the adoption agency that placed Liddy. She told me the name, but I can't remember it. It was a woman's name."

"Holly House."

"That's right. Thanks." He wrote it down, so he wouldn't forget it.

"How's it going?"

"I miss her." His voice shook a bit. "But I can't change who I am, ya know. I never expected to be rejected based on my last name." He hadn't really wanted to talk about it because it hurt too damn much. "Listen, she doesn't know I'm doing this. So, please don't say anything."

"You got it. Take it easy, Luke." The line went dead.

Luke called right away and spoke with a frantic woman on the other end. He didn't entirely understand what she said, but he gathered one thing: operations were about to cease if a lawyer didn't help file government paperwork.

He ran a hand through his hair. He could only imagine what those people must be going through right now.

Hanging up, he punched the preset number for Harold Lawson, his family's attorney. He'd known the man since he was fourteen. "Harold."

"Luke!" He sounded surprised. "Long time no see! How are you?"

"I'm sorry to bother you on a Saturday, but I need your help." He went on to describe what he'd learned about Holly House and that if Harold could act immediately they could continue operations.

"Luke, I don't do much non-profit."

"I understand, but you know people who do. It's urgent, Harold, not to mention important to me. Bill me whatever you need to."

This was one of those rare occasions when the access to money paid off. Luke didn't need a lot of money; he'd fallen in love with the simple life. But today, he'd grab on to that pile of money without blinking an eye.

"Okay," the man sighed. "Let me make a few calls, see what they can do."

Luke relayed the information. "Keep me posted. Thanks, Harold." He disconnected the line.

All he could do now was put his faith in the smartest man he knew—Harold Lawson. After the dust settled, he could make his donation. This agency was important to Liddy, so it was important to him. With all this money sitting in his account, why not do some good?

LIDDY APPLIED HER favorite lipstick in the mirror, her car keys in the opposite hand, ready to leave for work. This morning required extra concealer to cover the bags under her eyes and a bit more eyeshadow to mask the redness. She planned to call Holly House on the way into work to find out if they'd heard anything from the multitude of lawyers.

The second she stepped outside her door, the humidity pressed in on her chest. Cold and humid, which meant rain wasn't far off. The cloud cover added more weight to her depression.

To mock her dismal mood, the street was decked out in Christmas decorations. The light poles wrapped in green garland, and twinkling lights framed business awnings all down the street. Red ribbon coiled around the stop sign at the end of the street to look like a candy cane.

For her, this holiday season would be anything but joyous.

Her phone buzzed.

She answered while going down the wet stairs to her car. "Please tell me you at least got some sleep, Nan?"

"We're saved!" The jubilant words nearly bounced out of the speakerphone.

Liddy gasped. "Tell me everything."

"Some attorney called me late last night saying he'd heard about our issues, and offered to take care of all the filing for us. For *free*."

"Oh, my gosh! Who?"

"Harold Lawson from some big firm in Manhattan. They have offices in San Francisco."

Liddy stopped, and narrowed her eyes. "You called a firm in New York?"

"No, I didn't. That's the thing. He called me. But I'll take it! A higher power intervened on this one, Liddy. To top it off, we just got a *big* donation. Through the same attorney's office."

"How...who...how much?" The words garbled in her brain. This was far too good to be true.

"The donor wanted to remain anonymous. But it's enough to cover our operating expenses for the next *decade*, Liddy!"

The keys slipped from her hand, along with her designer purse—landing in the grass median between the sidewalk and the street.

"I feel like I'm going to explode. I'm so excited! Please celebrate with me! I want to take everyone out to dinner!"

Tingles raced down her spine, and her reflection in the car window paled. "How did he even find out about us?"

"Why does it matter, Liddy?"

"What's the name of the law firm?"

Nancy's exasperated sigh drowned out the shuffling of papers. "You're such a killjoy. Lawson, Whitman, & Rigby."

Liddy chanted the words in her head, trying to remember. "The name doesn't ring a bell."

"You called a *million* law offices yesterday, right? Besides, it doesn't matter. Truly. This is our angel. This is what we prayed for." Her exuberance coming through the phone made Liddy smile. "The adoptions are saved!"

"You're right. It doesn't matter." She swallowed back the emotion, knowing what those children must be feeling right now. That inexplicable joy and relief. *Thank God.* "Yes, I'm in for dinner."

"Let me call everyone, and I'll text you the details." Nancy giggled. "Oh, my Lord, Liddy can you believe this?" She disconnected on a laugh.

Liddy chuckled as she walked to her car. Nancy was right. This was a good thing. She lifted her face to the dreary sky, on the verge of unloading a massive rainfall on her head.

"Thank you. Whoever is responsible, you're an angel. Thank you."

Chapter
EIGHTEEN

AFTER A WEEK of not seeing Liddy, Luke did what he'd accused her of—stalked her on social media.

He was miserable, he admitted it. Unfortunately, she hadn't posted a single thing—no ski pictures, no comments about an egomaniac ski instructor, or about the magical view of stars from a mountain.

Life sucks sometimes, Sawyer.

He finally met the woman of his dreams, the woman he could trust, and she was pissed about his wealth. Never expected *that* reaction.

First time for everything.

The irony of the situation was not lost to him. He'd spent so much effort protecting himself from rejection, only to have it boomerang back in his face.

He understood what she felt. Well, only a bit. He'd never thought that using his middle name was actually *concealing* himself from people. Or lying. But maybe she had a point there. Somehow knowing he was from money had destroyed her. He wasn't sure *how*, exactly, but trust was the major problem. And that was solely his fault.

He stared at the piece of paper on his desk, where he'd written Holly House's phone number. He'd even gone so far as to find Liddy's address, and wrote it down. But he'd done nothing else about it. Just stared at it all week.

Patrick walked into the instructor's office. "Bro, I haven't seen a single prank from you this week. You need to get over the Cali blonde, and charge the hill."

He looked at his friend of three years. "No inspiration, man. Besides, you popped all the bubble paper. No more fun left to be had."

"Come on, big guy." Patrick slapped him on the shoulder. "Let's go grab a beer. Or down a few shots, whatever makes you happy. I'll even *pay*."

"What would make me happy is if she'd walk through that door right now."

Patrick shook his head. "That's like asking Bode Miller to come out of retirement, man. Pipe dream."

His chest weighed even heavier. "Bode's got nothing on her. And she wasn't a pipe dream, she was real."

"I'm starting to worry about you, man."

Luke's phone danced across his desk. His father's picture popped up on the screen.

His blood pressure increased, just knowing what was coming.

Do I have the energy for this?

"I'll give you some privacy," Patrick said, and closed the door behind him.

Luke pressed the button. "Hey, Dad."

"It's been a while since we've talked. I was beginning to feel forgotten."

He spun the paper on the desk. "I figured you've been busy with work." *He's always busy with work.*

"Your mother and sister have told me they've spoken to you about this foundation thing. I thought I'd throw my hat into the ring for that discussion as well."

"Because I hadn't agreed to it. Would you be calling if I already had?"

"Ouch, Luke."

He cringed. "Sorry. That came out too harsh."

His father paused. "Luke, what's wrong?"

That question was enough for him to realize he really was out of it. Robert Daniel Rothchild had never asked his son that question in ten years. Probably because Luke had walked out of that ballroom, leaving his family to make their apologies for any *embarrassment* their son had caused. Showing weakness in public might as well have been tantamount to blasphemy in their eyes.

"Rough week, that's all." He grabbed the foam stress buffalo, and squeezed. The eyes bulged from the head.

"Your mother mentioned something about a woman."

"I never actually confirmed that."

His dad humphed. "Which tells me it's true. And based

on the sound of your voice, it didn't end well."

"Are you going to try and use this in your negotiating tactic to get me to move back to New York? I'm sorry, Dad. But I can't work for you."

"No. I gave up on that idea a year after you moved out there."

He dropped the buffalo. "What? Then why does Mom—"

"Do you blame any mother for wanting her children to live close by? It was never about the role, Luke. Forgive us for wanting to *share* in your life and what makes you happy. We're a bit selfish that way."

Luke stared at the buffalo painting on the wall, stunned. He'd never imagined in all these years his father would ever utter those words. *It was never about the role.*

"Your mother really does need a break from running the foundation. It's become too much for her. We honestly thought it would be a perfect fit for you, but you don't have to do it if you don't want to. Your sister will kill me for saying that. Bottom line, we miss you. It would be nice to see you more than twice a year."

That nearly brought a tear to Luke's eye. "I'd like that, too." He missed his family greatly, but their inner circle made it nearly impossible to enjoy their company. The attitude didn't match how Luke wanted to live his life. Maybe the foundation would give him the closeness to his family he craved, but provide enough distance from that brutal mentality of the Rothchild business.

"So, tell me about this woman," his father asked. "How can I help?"

He pressed his lips together, hating the words about to come out of his mouth. "You actually can't. It's too late."

"Why? Did something happen? Has she died?" The question came out sincere.

"No."

"Then it's never too late, son. Just show her who you really are."

"I did." He tossed the paper with Liddy's address in the trash. "That's why it's too late."

❆❆❆

THE CABLE CAR jostled up the hill as Liddy opened a piece of mail, on her way from work to lunch with the girls. There was no parking near that area of downtown, and the iconic mode of transportation stopped right where she needed anyway.

The return address on the envelope made her cringe.

The resort doctor. It had been just over a week since leaving Colorado.

This was surely the expensive bill for her ankle sprain during vacation.

Like I needed the reminder of him.

She scowled through the list of charges, line item by line item.

Until she read the bottom of the bill, with a small red

stamp, PAID IN FULL.

"Huh?" she asked aloud.

A woman in the bench next to her glanced her way, but didn't say anything.

Liddy rubbed her forehead. She couldn't imagine she'd hit her deductible with her health insurance—let alone the out of pocket maximum, where her plan would cover one hundred percent.

Nothing else came with the paper. No explanation, or receipt.

The bell dinged overhead, signaling an upcoming stop. The restaurant was only a block ahead.

She shoved the letter back in the envelope and then in her purse to figure out later.

When the cable car stopped, she stepped off, barely flinching at the ache in her ankle. Her snug, knee-high leather boots provided additional support.

The patio of *Le Cafe* was empty, even during the busy lunch hour because no one wanted to sit outside when it was below seventy.

Liddy walked right through the doors of the eatery that was their favorite place when they wanted a delicious, cheap lunch. She spotted the girls being shown to their usual square table in the back.

"I'm so glad you called us. We were starting to worry." Sam hugged her, then shrugged out of her camel-colored coat, and slung it over the back of her chair. Yet again, so stylish.

"How're you doing?" Jordan asked. "You've been uncharacteristically distant."

Today, the restaurant played muted, overly-cheerful Christmas music. Fitting, with the holly wreaths on the doors, and the pictures covered in wrapping paper and fancy bows.

But far too happy for Liddy.

"I'm okay," she sighed. "One day at a time." She adjusted the cowl on her oversized gray sweater, comfortable yet still fashionable with her leggings and boots. She'd worn a lot of gray this week. Even her boss had mentioned that.

Jordan and Sam exchanged sideways glances, but Liddy didn't care. She knew enough to realize she and Luke didn't have a future. She was merely a plaything for the cocky ski instructor. Okay, well, that might be a bit extreme. Perhaps he did really like her, but she wouldn't survive his family's scrutiny.

Time to stop thinking about him.

"Has your ankle been giving you any problems?" Jordan asked. Always the coach.

"A little stiff on cold mornings like today, but stretching helps. And coffee." She forced a smile and sipped on her latte.

"So, tell us," Sam leaned her elbows on the table. "What have you been doing this week? Working, or volunteering at Holly House?"

Her eyebrows raised on that question. "I do have some good news about Holly House. They almost lost their certification."

Jordan sputtered over her ice water. "What? That's *good* news?"

"Yeah. *Almost* lost it. But didn't."

"Girl, you're crazy," Sam chimed in, wrinkles creasing her forehead.

The waiter approached the table to take their orders. Liddy didn't have much of an appetite these days, but she ordered a salad with dressing on the side. If she didn't finish it, at least she could take it home.

After the waiter left, Jordan said, "You have to explain this."

"Holly House received a letter from the Department of Consumer Affairs. *Weeks* ago, but they found the letter lost in a drawer, thanks to their retired admin. They needed to renew their certification to remain open to conduct adoptions—but an attorney has to do the filing and everything. Well, come to find out," she rolled her eyes for effect, "stinkin' law firms aren't open on Saturday. Not even an emergency number."

"No, everyone has their attorney's personal cell number for that." Sam made it sound so obvious.

"Yeah, well, we didn't know that. So, I'm calling around last Saturday, leaving a bunch of messages all over the state. One finally called back, from New York, of all places. And," she rounded her eyes, because it truly was exciting, "the law firm said they were forwarding an anonymous donation to the House, too. *Massive* donation. I can't believe how fortunate everything turned out." She shook her head just thinking how close they'd come to losing it all. "Saved two adoptions last week." She finished the tale with a smile.

Jordan and Sam sent glances at each other again.

"What the hell is going on between you two? Do I have something on my face?"

Jordan licked her lips. "Interestingly enough, Luke called me last Saturday."

Her heart turned over just hearing his name. "What?!"

"He asked for the name of your adoption agency, because he couldn't remember it. He claimed he wanted to make a donation." Jordan visibly held her breath.

Liddy slumped in her chair, processing the news. "A donation?" She wasn't sure if she'd said that aloud or in her head. "Of course. The law firm was from New York." *Where the Rothchild family lives.*

Jordan and Sam stared, sitting quietly, waiting for her response.

Liddy swallowed. "That has to be the nicest thing anyone has ever done for me." Which probably meant he was the one who'd paid her medical bill, too. "That asshole."

Sam coughed into her napkin. Jordan bit her lips between her teeth.

"We were sworn to secrecy."

"Ha! He doesn't know you can't keep a secret for shit." Liddy laughed.

Sam smirked. Soon the whole table nearly fell out of their chairs laughing.

"Okay, so what does this mean?" Sam asked.

"I guess it means I need to give that jerk a chance."

"I'll drink to that." Jordan raised her water glass.

The next move was Liddy's, the only question was *What*?

"I think this Christmas music is actually growing on me."

Chapter NINETEEN

HOLIDAY MUSIC BLARED over the speakers throughout the Lodge nearly non-stop since Thanksgiving. A rock version of "Jingle Bells" played every half-hour and rattled around in Luke's head like an annoying commercial.

All the guests wore smiles, with the special energy around Christmas time, never mind it was still weeks away. The jovial demeanor was so easy for them at a place like Buffalo Ridge Resort.

Luke had to fake his.

He finished renting out skis to a newlywed couple, and checked the roster of his upcoming beginners class. They were busier than ever with a fresh layer of snow the night before.

The rental shop was briefly empty, and he was finally able to take his first deep breath. Through the window, sun glimmered off the slopes, and the pine trees never looked so green topped with fresh white powder.

Skier's paradise mocked him—because he was living in his own custom bell jar of misery.

He started to empty the trash can under the counter.

"I'd like to sign up for ski lessons."

Luke froze. He knew that voice. The melodious, and equally smart-ass, voice.

He stood, his heart nearly bursting at Liddy's angelic form staring at him from the front of the room. Her merlot cable-knit sweater matched her lipstick, her blonde curls loose around her shoulders.

He waited a few seconds to make sure she was real. That he wasn't hallucinating. "Okay. Do you have any ski experience?"

She moved forward, slowly, casually . . . checking out the displays on the walls. "Yes. Unfortunately, the last time I tried, I crashed."

His heart raced faster with each step she took. "I see. Didn't exactly work out for you," he pried, hoping against all hope they had a chance.

Liddy finally reached the counter, and leaned her hip against it. "Best five days of my life."

He swallowed hard, his mouth nearly drooling from her delicate, sweet perfume. Deep in his heart, he had to believe she would feel that way. But now that she stood in front of him, saying those words out loud, he was sure he had to be dreaming.

"Looking to have a similar experience." She stood tall, and held out her hand. "Let's start over. I'm Lydia Michelle Drake. Call me Liddy. I have a less than ideal past, but it's made me who I am today."

He couldn't hold back his smile if his life depended on it. Her soft hand felt like the down of a new pillow in his. "I'm Luke Sawyer Rothchild. Head ski bum-slash-instructor, egotistical prankster, and irredeemably in love with you."

Her eyebrows rose, the corner of her mouth daring to pull up. "I think you've more than redeemed yourself for every single slight you might've done." A glossy sheen filled her eyes. "Your donation."

His heart sank a little. "So, you're saying the money brought you back here."

She shook her head. "The gesture. You found out what was important to me, and helped those in need. All the money in the world can't compete with that."

His soul inflated with those words, and nearly burst. He moved in closer, curling her hand against his chest. Right over his heart.

"I didn't expect you to come back. No one's surprised me in a very long time, and you keep doing that."

She brushed a stray hair away from his face. "At least you know I'm not boring."

"Boring or not, I'll take you any way I can. As long as it's *me* you want."

Liddy pressed her lips to his, so sweet and tender, she stole his breath. When she pulled back, the sheen in her eyes doubled. "Well, ski bum, I can't help that I've fallen in love with you."

He grinned, and called over his shoulder. "Rachel, I'm outta here. You got it?"

A woman with a skier's tan and short brown hair poked her head out between two rows of hanging skis. "Yeah. I got it. Thanks for the help during the rush."

Still holding Liddy's hand, Luke led her out of the ski shop to his empty office. He yanked her close, shut the door, and fused his lips to hers.

"Shit, I missed you," he breathed over her mouth.

"I missed you."

"These last nine days have been miserable without you."

"For me, too." She nibbled her lower lip and peered up at him. "Luke, I'm scared."

He craned his neck back to meet her gaze directly. "Scared of what?"

"Scared your family won't like me . . . because of my past."

"You're devoted to foster kids and charity. I think my mother will be doing back handsprings over you. Don't sell yourself short." He stroked the side of her face because she felt so good in his arms.

Her lips curved up again.

"Besides, my siblings think I'm an arrogant prick—"

"You are."

He chuckled. "So, you'll be a trip to Disney and winning the lotto all rolled into one. They'll love you."

"I've screwed up so many relationships, I don't want to

ruin this one, too." She tightened her hold on his waist. "Tell me when I'm being too clingy, or becoming boring."

Luke brushed back a curl from her cheek, her angelic face too irresistible. "Only if you promise to tell me when I'm being a jackass."

She grinned, and her eyes twinkled just as he'd remembered.

"Come with me, baby."

Holding onto her hand, she followed him to the employee residence building. The gravel path leading up the hill to his room crunched under his boots, his chest about to burst. He couldn't believe she was here. She'd actually come back. He wanted every second with her he could spare. But on a Sunday afternoon, too many people were around. For what he had planned, he wanted her all to himself, with no one else to bother them.

He reached up to the top shelf in his closet and grabbed two wool blankets. "Sweet cheeks, we're going outside. Do you trust me?"

LIDDY SWALLOWED HARD. Surely, she heard that wrong. "Outside? It's like thirty-five degrees."

He swung an arm around her and pulled her close in that sexy, possessive way he'd mastered. "I promise to keep you warm."

The adventurous side he brought out of her made her answer the only thing that came to her mind. "Yes."

He grinned from ear to ear. They walked back outside, and strolled away from the resort, into the trees.

Tall pine trees climbed higher the deeper they went, the evergreen scent surrounding them. The sounds of the skiers in the distance grew more muffled the farther they climbed, until she couldn't hear them anymore.

"Do you know where we're going?"

"Baby, I know every tree, stump, rock, and mogul of this place." He stopped and grinned. "We're going where we can be as loud as we want, and no one will hear."

She inhaled. *Oh, my.* She never had a man so in-charge, so wholly masculine that she could so blindly trust. He would take her to the edge of danger and hold her tight, and she'd love every minute of it.

After another five minutes, he pushed through some lower hanging branches, and revealed a small area, bare of trees. Beneath a thin layer of snow, green grass poked up, shielded from most of the snow drifts. A perfect little natural getaway.

"A few years ago, a lightning strike burned this section of the gorge." He opened his arms to the clearing and took a deep breath. "Now, it's a tiny paradise in the mountains."

"And what are we doing here?"

He didn't answer her. He moved in front of her, as if blocking the rest of the trees from looking at her. Then he unzipped her jacket and slipped his arms inside, around her waist and pulled her close.

Tingles raced all along her spine, up into her neck, and down into her sex.

He claimed her mouth with his—sensual, slow, and thorough.

Liddy draped her arms around his neck. His kisses were like coming home.

He broke his hold, just when her body began to crave more. He whipped off his down jacket, and pulled his sweatshirt over his head.

Goosebumps rose up on his skin instantly in the cold air, but *damn*, still so delectable.

She nearly drooled.

He slipped his jacket back on, leaving it open. Bare skin exposed to the elements.

Then, he spread a wool blanket out and folded his sweatshirt in the second blanket.

There was no hope in stopping herself. She placed her hands on his chest, stroking along every plane and ridge, loving the warmth that radiated off his skin.

"Your turn, beautiful." He pushed off her jacket and tucked it under his arm. Then lifted her sweater.

The cold air against her bare stomach tightened everything in her body, making the earlier arousal fade instantly.

"Hang on," he chuckled, and made quick work of her bra.

This is a bad idea.

The straps came loose, and he pulled the satin away.

"Oh, hell!" The cold grew colder, hitting her nipples faster than a bullet train.

"Bear with me." He draped her jacket around her shoulders, and she slipped her arms in.

He stuffed her clothes in the folded wool blanket. Then, hauled her close, skin to skin.

Her teeth had started to chatter by the time his heat rubbed into her belly, warming the rest of her. She didn't have long to think about the cold, since his mouth moved against hers, claiming her. Almost branding her with his scent.

Her insides melted.

"I've thought about bringing you out here, naked on the snow, since the moment I laid eyes on you."

She grinned.

"This is the perfect time, too. We won't get another opportunity since I'm moving."

She stepped back and yanked her jacket closed. "You're moving?"

His eyes turned confused. "I didn't tell you?"

She gawked at him. "No! I would've remembered that. Where are you going?"

He stepped forward, closing the gap between them. "San Francisco."

Her heart stopped. Actually stopped. It must have, because she couldn't catch her breath.

His smile widened. "I can't very well expect you to move here when your whole life's there."

"You're coming to Cali." The words came out slowly, not sure she heard him correctly.

"I'm going wherever you are," he said softly over her lips. He gave her one last deep-reaching kiss, and helped lay her back on the wool blanket.

"And before coming in Cali, we'll cum here . . ." His hands brushed down her naked torso and gently toyed with her breasts. "A lot."

"Mmm."

He laid kisses down her neck, over her clavicle, to her areolas and nipples. He suckled, laved, and bit.

"Oh," she called out, the electricity shooting down to her sex.

The mixture of intense heat from his mouth on her skin with the frigid air following his wake intensified the building surge of energy in her body.

As he continued, her wetness grew, and her face flushed with excitement. With anticipation. She writhed and moaned under his torment.

"Luke," she pleaded.

He only glanced up and smiled. His kisses traveled down her tummy, dipping into her navel. Then with a fingertip just under her waistband, he teased her, kissing and licking, her leggings barely budging.

Her fingers wove through his hair, squirming under his oh-so-slow movement.

With his free hand, he bent her leg, pulling at her boot

laces. He repeated the action to the opposite leg.

His words fluttered over her belly. "Baby, are you ready to get completely naked?"

She was cold and insanely hot at the same time. She didn't care so much about the temperature, she just needed to come. "Yes," she begged.

He leaned up, popped off her boots, and removed her thong and leggings, tossing them in the pile.

She lay before him, naked save for her ski jacket. Before he could make another move, she sat up and yanked on his jeans to pull her mouth to his chest. "You taste divine."

She worked his jeans free enough to reach inside and caress his hard cock—harder than she'd ever remembered. The tip glistened with pre-cum, pleading for attention. She couldn't help herself. She leaned lower and quickly gave him a quick swipe with her tongue.

He gripped her shoulders and growled. "You'll pay for that."

He pushed her back down, pulled off his jacket, and commanded, "Legs over my shoulders."

The playful fire in his eyes made her heart skip more. She did as he asked.

He flipped the jacket over them as he leaned down and claimed her pussy.

Sparks of energy rebounded in her body. "Oh, God, Luke."

"Christ, Liddy, you're soaked."

He laved her lips, scraping her arousal over her clit and around again. His hands stretched to her breasts, covering them with his warm hands. He played with her nipples, tugging and twisting.

She was so close, any second she'd explode. Right off that edge she craved.

He pulled back.

"What are doing?" she shrieked.

He retrieved a condom from his back pocket and grinned. "Just being a good boy scout."

"Asshole," she muttered.

He only chuckled as he returned to her sex, making love to her with his mouth, but never letting her tip over. He was edging her.

Asshole. Fucking, sexy, addictive asshole.

She writhed, needing to come in the worst way.

His tongue gently stroked her delicate lips, avoiding her clit, as his fingers tugged at her nipples.

Her legs spread further apart, causing the jacket to slide down his back. She lifted her hips, aching for more. But he only chuckled, backing off anytime she tried to increase the pressure.

The liquid heat drifted down to her ass cheeks.

Whenever he felt her get close, he'd back off. Then start again, up and around, gently licking and barely poking inside.

"Please, Luke."

He pulled one of his hands down from her breast and

drove two fingers inside her, and pressed his tongue to her clit, massaging.

"Ah!" she screamed. "Luke." The orgasm crashed over her, rocketing through her body from the inside out. Her back bowed, and she cried out again, echoing off the trees overhead.

When she was calm enough to open her eyes, she lowered her legs. Luke sheathed himself with a condom, his whole body glistening from sweat. Or maybe from her, she couldn't tell.

He slipped on his jacket, and as he commanded, "Over," he lifted her, and turned her to rest on all fours.

Smack!

"Ow!" The sting bit into her ass and spread out along her skin. "What was that for?"

"Because I can."

Smack! This time, a mild burn followed the sting she relished.

She moaned. *I really do like it kinky.*

With a growl, Luke dove into her.

He flung her jacket over her head. If her hands weren't planted, the coat would've gone sailing.

He covered her, his whole front warming her backside. "And because you left. You don't get to leave again," he whispered in her ear.

She panted. "You sure that's what you want?"

He kissed her neck and shoulder, gently biting her body

like it was a delicious meal. "Absolutely. Promise me you'll never leave again." His hips pumped into her, the rhythm picking up, drawing on another orgasm.

"I promise. I swear."

He thrust harder and faster.

The cold didn't matter, the fear of being caught in the open didn't matter. Just this intensity, this burning throb that filled up her soul, meant everything. If she could hold onto this all-consuming need . . .

"Oh, Luke. You feel so good. You don't get to leave me."

"I promise. I swear."

Another sensational climax exploded, tugging him in deeper so he could release inside her. Both of them bound together by some inexplicable desire. A love that she prayed would blossom more each day.

They collapsed on the blanket, breathing heavily. Quickly he pulled out and tugged her jacket back over her. Then he reached for the clothes, dropped them on their legs and covered them with the second blanket.

They lay side by side, his arm around her, staring at each other, sated and happier than anybody had the right to be.

"At some point, I want to do this again. Only under those stars. Look into your eyes as you come. Bring a whole new meaning to explosions in the sky."

She grinned against him. "I can't believe you had me completely naked out here," she said softly.

"That was so hot. Your creamy, soft skin against the

snow. I should have taken a picture."

Her eyes rolled to the heavens. "You're crazy."

"I'm crazy in love with you, Liddy." His eyes read sincere. Then turned sorrowful. "Please, don't let money get between us."

The words tugged at her heart. She never wanted to bring him pain.

"I love you, Luke." She pushed him to his back and straddled his waist. "And, I don't care about the money. It's the hot monkey-sex I can't live without."

He grinned as he reached for her head, pulling her to his lips. The place where heaven and earth collided.

Thank you for reading the Sweet Escape series. As a special treat for our readers, we wrote a series epilogue!

If you've finished all three books in the series, please read the finale at BookFunnel, our gift to you!

BookHip.com/TPLQQX

A Message FROM THE AUTHORS

Thank you so much for reading the series!

If you enjoyed this story and the series, please consider posting a review at one or more of your favorite retailers, as well as Goodreads. Even a short review, one or two lines, can be a tremendous help and encouragement to the authors. Your review is also a gift to other readers who may be searching for just this sort of story,

and will be grateful you helped them find it.

Thank you!

Mia London & Susan Sheehey

About THE AUTHORS

Mia London

Mia London loves to write.

After reading fiction for years, she decided it was finally time to put those images and scenes floating around in her head down on paper.

She is a huge fan of romance, highly optimistic, and wildly faithful to the HEA (happily ever after). Her goal is to create a fantasy you will enjoy with characters you could love.

She lives in Texas with her attentive, loving, supermodel husband, and perfectly behaved, brilliant children. Her produce never wilts, there are no weeds in her flowerbeds, and chocolate is her favorite food group.

www.Facebook.com/MiaLondonAuthor
Twitter- @MiaLondonAuthor
Webpage- www.MiaLondon.com
Email- mia@mialondon.com

Susan Sheehey writes contemporary romance and romantic suspense adventure. Water plays a crucial element in all her novels, and she's a strong advocate for Autism awareness and acceptance. She squeezes in writing time between chauffeuring around her two boys, and guzzling down French Vanilla coffee. Her beloved husband keeps her relatively sane, and full of laughter. She and her family live in Texas.

www.SusanSheehey.com
www.Facebook.com/SusanSheehey
www.Twitter.com/SusieQWriter
www.Pinterest.com/SusanSheehey

Join her newsletter for monthly announcements, updates, ARC requests, and special giveaways!

https://landing.mailerlite.com/webforms/landing/p5b0i9